Joseph Hansen

Joseph Hansen wrote nearly forty novels in the course of a long career, but is best known for the ground-breaking series of twelve Dave Brandstetter crime novels. Brandstetter was a pioneering character: a tough private eye and happily uncloseted gay man. Hansen was an active campaigner for equal rights (though he disliked the word "gay" and always described himself as "homosexual"). He founded the pioneering gay journal *Tangents* in 1965, hosted a radio show called *Homosexuality Today*, and was involved in setting up the first Gay Pride parade in Hollywood in 1970, the same year that the first Brandstetter novel was published. In 1992, he won a Lifetime Achievement Award from the Private Eye Writers of America. He died in 2004.

JOSEPH HANSEN

Fadeout

**MULHOLLAND
BOOKS**

HODDER

This paperback edition first published in Great Britain in
2015 by Mulholland Books
An imprint of Hodder & Stoughton
An Hachette UK company

3

A CIP catalogue record for this title is available from the
British Library

Paperback ISBN 978 1 444 78447 3
eBook ISBN 978 1 444 78446 6

Typeset in Plantin Light by
Palimpsest Book Production Ltd, Falkirk, Stirlingshire

Printed and bound by Clays Ltd, St Ives plc

Hodder & Stoughton policy is to use papers that are natural,
renewable and recyclable products and made from wood
grown in sustainable forests. The logging and manufacturing
processes are expected to conform to the environmental
regulations of the country of origin.

Hodder & Stoughton Ltd
338 Euston Road
London NW1 3BH

www.hodder.co.uk

Fadeout

I

Fog shrouded the canyon, a box canyon above a California ranch town called Pima. It rained. Not hard but steady and gray and dismal. Shaggy pines loomed through the mist like threats. Sycamores made white, twisted gestures above the arroyo. Down the arroyo water pounded, ugly, angry and deep. The road shouldered the arroyo. It was a bad road. The rains had chewed its edges. There were holes. Mud and rock half buried it in places. It was steep and winding and there were no guard rails.

He drove it with sweating hands. Why? His smile was sour. Why so careful? Wasn't death all he'd wanted for the past six weeks? His mouth tightened. That was finished. He'd made up his mind to live now. Hadn't he? Live and forget—at least until he could remember without pain. And that would happen someday. Sure it would. All the books said so. The sum of human wisdom. Meantime, he was working again.

And here was the bridge. It was wooden, maybe thirty feet in span, ten feet wide. Heavy beams, thick planks, big iron bolts. Simple and strong. The right kind of bridge for this place. He stopped the car and got out. Cold. He shivered and hunched his

I

shoulders. The rain laid a quick, eager surface on the road. It splashed over his shoes. His feet were wet when he walked out on the bridge.

Its railings on the downstream side had been replaced. The new two-by-fours looked pale. They still bled sap. A car had smashed out the old ones. He shoved his hands into the pockets of his trench coat and stood staring down. There was a lot of raw power to that water. It was muddy and seething, so he couldn't see the boulders tumbling, but he could hear them, feel them. The bridge vibrated. That water could tumble a car as easily. It had. Five days ago. Three days later, when there was a letup in the storm and the water level fell, police had found the car. A mile downstream. Battered, flattened, glass smashed out, doors half torn off. They hadn't found the driver.

That was why Dave Brandstetter was here.

He walked to the far side of the bridge, where the road angled off and climbed steeply. It was a hell of an unsafe arrangement. But the whole road was unsafe, no more than a poorly paved deer track. Still, no one used it but the few people who lived in the canyon. Knowing it, they didn't fear it. Which could have been a mistake. At least for one of them. On a night of rain and darkness, Fox Olson's white Thunderbird might have hit the top of that slope too fast. It had certainly hit the bottom too fast.

Dave slogged back to his car.

He found the house a mile beyond the bridge. It stood back and up from the road under towering, ragged-barked eucalyptus trees. The dark ivy that covered the slope in front was glossed by rain. So were the two cars in the drive—new red Mustang, battered old Chevy. He left his own car under a manzanita by the road. The house was one-story, rambling, sided with cedar shakes that hadn't been painted and hadn't had time yet really to weather. The place looked comfortable and expensive. He pressed the button beside the front door.

The woman who opened it was small, not much above five feet. Thin, fine-boned, in her early forties, like himself. Her hair was brown with some gray in it. She had cropped it like a boy's, smart and simple. Her hips were narrow as a boy's and looked right in the brown corduroy Levi's. She wore a brown checked wool shirt. No jewelry, no makeup except lipstick. She couldn't have looked more feminine.

"Mrs. Olson?" he said. "I'm Dave Brandstetter."

"And soaking wet," she apologized. "I'm sorry about that. Come in." With a glance at the weather and a shiver, she shut the door. "Give me those and I'll hang them in the kitchen to drip. You go make yourself comfortable."

She took the trench coat and canvas hat away. He stepped down into the living room. It was long. Pitched roof, hand-hewn beams, knotty-pine paneling. Logs blazed in a fieldstone fireplace flanked by loaded bookshelves. He took a wing chair close to the fire, hoping his feet would dry. Above the fireplace hung a big painting. He couldn't quite make it out—some kind of white trestle thing rearing up nightmarish against a black sky.

3

"What is it?" he asked her when she came in.

"Fox painted it. Quite recently. It's very different from anything else he ever did. It's called 'The Chute.' He won't—wouldn't tell me what it means. He just says, 'It's a memory.'"

A bottle of brandy warmed on the hearth. Christian Brothers. She poured splashes from it into two small snifters, handed him one and sat down across from him, feet tucked under her. On the coffee table between them, the mechanism of a lighter glinted in a burl of polished wood. When he set a cigarette in his mouth and reached for the lighter, she got it first and worked the flame for him. Automatically. Habit. Nothing meant. Except, evidently, that she had lit her husband's cigarettes. Funny. She wasn't the type. Not mousy enough. Not mousy at all.

"Thank you," he said.

She sat back and gave a little businesslike smile. "Now, what's this all about, Mr. Brandstetter?"

"Routine." He smiled back.

"You said that on the phone. What does it mean?"

"That my company—every insurance company— sends out investigators in cases like this."

"Like this?"

"Where the policyholder's body can't be found."

"Can't be—" She blinked. "Oh, but it will be. I'm sure it will. When the storm's over."

"There was a lull in the storm day before yesterday," he said. "They were able to find the car—"

"And have you seen that car?" she asked.

4

"Yes. This morning. At the police garage."

"And you drove up here just now. Which means you've seen the force of the water in the arroyo. Does it seem strange to you that Fox's body wasn't in that car?"

"No. But it ought to have been in the arroyo." The ashtray was black Mexican pottery. He put ashes into it carefully. "Twenty men searched for it. Police, sheriffs. They didn't find it, Mrs. Olson."

"I know," she said quietly. "I was with them . . . But at the foot of the canyon is a storm drain that carries the arroyo water under the town to the river."

"A body reaching a storm drain," he said, "would be caught in the gratings."

A corner of her mouth tightened in a kind of smile. "Have you been in that storm drain, Mr. Brandstetter?"

"In it?" He raised an eyebrow. "No. Have you?"

"Many times. I played there as a child. It was built when I was about ten. Before that the arroyo itself cut right through Pima. Every time there was a storm like this, it nearly washed the town away. Lloyd Chalmers built the drain. It was his first big job. He was just starting out in the contracting business. He couldn't have been much older than twenty. He's the mayor now, in his fourth term. My husband is running against him. Was."

"I know." The posters were pasted up all over Pima, flaring reds and oranges, paper wrinkled in the rain. CHALMERS . . . GROWTH. Rugged, white-maned man. OLSON . . . HONESTY. Laughing man

5

with thinning blond hair. "I've seen the posters. You were telling me about the storm drain."

"Well, we children used to play in it, as I say. It's huge and shadowy and cool. And of course, in summer, dry and completely safe. But there are no gratings, Mr. Brandstetter. It's simply a concrete tunnel. Oh, there are overhead gratings, from the streets. But cross gratings would only defeat the drain's purpose. They'd be choked with debris in no time."

Dave nodded. "Scrub, tree branches—yes, I can see that. But it's that sort of material that ought to have caught and held your husband's body in the arroyo itself. Someplace in the four or five miles between the bridge and town." He swallowed his brandy. "The police agree with me. A human body is a heavy, clumsy, floppy thing. A dead body. With clothes to snag. It should have been in the arroyo."

"Well, it wasn't." She got up for the brandy bottle. "Which means that Fox—" But she couldn't manage that. She stood with her back to him, rigid, for a minute. When she turned it was abruptly and her voice was harsh. "The body was swept through the drain into the river. That's all. He'll be found after the storm, when the water level falls. Of course he will." She put an inch of brandy into his glass and her own. Her hand shook.

"Maybe," he said. "My company doesn't think so."

"What in the world do they think?"

"They won't know what to think till I'm through."

She set the bottle back on the hearth. It clinked. "And when will that be?"

6

"After I've asked a lot of questions."

"Captain Herrera asked a good many. Couldn't you—"

"I've talked to Captain Herrera."

"I was honest." She managed a dry smile and she was in control of her voice again. But when she sat down this time she kept her feet on the floor. "No, Fox wasn't sober, not quite. He was on his way to KPIM to tape some commercials. He hated them. Kept putting them off. That was why he left so late. But . . . he'd driven this canyon many times less sober. When my father stayed here sick and we'd come back from a late party, for example, Fox would drive the nurse home and not even remember it the next morning."

Dave interrupted her. "I wasn't going to ask whether he was drunk."

"No?" She frowned and tilted her head. "Well, then, perhaps you think he committed suicide? You're going to ask me if he was worried about money."

"He wasn't. I've checked with the bank."

"Well, then, his health. Had he told me of some awful pains he was having—?" She broke off. "What's wrong?"

Bright and fierce he pictured again Rod's face, clay-white, fear in the eyes, as he'd seen it when he found him in the glaring bathroom that first night of the horrible months that had ended in his death from intestinal cancer.

"Sorry." He got up quickly, blindly, and walked down the long room to stare out the glass doors

7

into the flagged patio, rocks and moss, where rain wept into a dark lily pond under mournful ferns. He said savagely, "No, I'm not going to ask you questions like that. Because I don't think your husband had an accident, Mrs. Olson. I don't think he committed suicide. I don't even"—he swung around to look at her—"I don't even think he's dead."

She was facing him, standing. Her mouth sagged open. She looked the way people her age, his age, wish they didn't when they see themselves in the bathroom mirror first thing in the morning. "What did you say?"

"I think he shifted that white T-bird of his into neutral at the top of that slope down to the bridge, stepped out, let the hand brake go, watched the car crash into the arroyo, and then walked off and didn't come back."

"But why? Why should he do such a thing?"

Dave shrugged. "That's what I'm here to find out."

"But . . . that's mad. You can't be serious." She almost laughed at him. "You honestly believe, because poor Fox's body can't be found, that he—he and I"—she groped for words—"have concocted some James M. Cain sort of scheme to collect his life insurance?"

"It's one explanation," Dave said. "A hundred thousand dollars is a lot of money, Mrs. Olson."

"Not enough," she said, and stopped smiling. "If Fox Olson were alive, he'd be here, Mr. Brandstetter. And I'm going to show you why." She came toward him, her mouth tight with scorn, her eyes looking straight and hard into his. She slid back the glass door to the patio. Cold wet air came in. She nodded and he stepped out into it and she followed him and shut the door behind her. "Come with me, please. We'll clear this nonsense up right now."

The deep eaves of the house formed a sheltered walkway around the patio. Then they were in the rain, climbing flagged steps between rock-walled flower beds under Japanese maples. Fallen leaves clung to his shoes. Sheltered again, this time by the overhang of a shake-sided cabana, they passed the swimming pool, rain whispering into it. At the far end of the pool, a tall hedge of bamboo partly hid a two-story double garage. They climbed its outside stairs. The door at the top wasn't locked. She swung it open.

He heard Fox Olson's voice singing inside.

9

2

In the Daffodil Café in Pima, where he'd stopped
for coffee this morning after the long wet drive from
L.A., that voice had come from a nine-dollar radio
on top of a refrigerator. The pudgy, white-haired
woman in starched yellow gingham, tending the
counter, had stood in front of him with the glass
coffeepot forgotten in her hand, while she listened,
her faded blue eyes staring far away.

Wanting the coffee, he'd naturally paid attention
to what she was listening to so hard. A catchy,
forgettable little Western song. Guitar, clip-clop
hoofbeats. Mild baritone. Pleasant, whimsical
delivery. But nothing special. Yet tears were running
down her soft old cheeks when the song ended.
With a sad little smile she shook her head as she
poured Dave's coffee.

"Wasn't he wonderful?" she sighed.

"Who's that?" Dave hadn't heard the announcer.

"Who!" She was indignant. "Why, Fox, Fox
Olson, of course. Who'd you think?"

"I didn't know." Dave smiled apology.

"Then you must be a stranger," she said.

"I am." He tried the coffee. It was good. He lit a
cigarette. "I gather Fox Olson's a local celebrity."

"Was," she said. "Oh, we miss him. The day they stop playing his songs . . . Well, you know, they tried. Right after he was killed in that car crash up the canyon. They just stopped playing him. As though we was such hicks we didn't know there's such a thing as tapes these days. Like now he was gone, we wasn't going to hear him no more.

"But everybody hollered so. Oh, I tell you, Pima kicked up a fuss. I don't expect there was anybody in town, except Mayor Chalmers, of course, that didn't phone up KPIM"—she said it as if it were a name, not call letters—"and say, put Fox Olson back on the radio. Well, they did. They got recordings of all his old broadcasts. They keep playing parts of those. They better." Her jowls set firmly, she turned and banged the coffeepot back on its hot plate. "They better not stop. . . ."

Out of the radio the voice had sounded tinny. Here, now, in the rain, on the slatted wooden landing at the top of the garage stairs, hearing it through the open door, it sounded real. It wasn't. It was a recording. Ten-inch reels turned on a big professional tape rig against the wall opposite the door. Stainless steel panels, knobs, dials. Black speaker cones next to the ceiling. Once inside the room he could hear tape hiss. But for a moment there he'd have sworn he heard a living man.

A girl in blue sat at a big, sleek, clean-lined desk. Her hands were on the keys of a new electric typewriter but they were still. She was sitting with her face turned up, listening, wearing the same rapt expression as the old Daffodil waitress. Only her eyes were shut and she was young and her face was like a flower with rain blessing it. Had been, for an instant. Then Mrs. Olson shut the door, crossed the room and struck a switch and the voice slurred and died. The girl opened her eyes, startled blue.

"I wish you wouldn't, Terry. I've asked you before."

"I'm sorry, Thorne." The girl was very blond. She blushed like a white rose. "You said you had an appointment. I didn't think you'd be coming out."

"Neither did I. And I apologize for interrupting your . . . work." Thorne Olson eyed skeptically the half-typed page in the machine, the heap of mimeographed scripts on the desk. "But I felt it was important for Mr. Brandstetter, here, to see Fox's studio." Her smile at Dave was mechanical. She gestured, already turning away. "Miss Lockridge, my husband's secretary." She crossed the room to a small, glossy bar, where she found brandy and two more little snifters. She said, "Tell him what you're working on, would you, Terry?"

"Why . . ." The girl had a nice, shy, high-school smile. Her voice was a whisper. "It's a book. Of Fox's—Mr. Olson's stories. He used to tell them on the air, read them. I'm typing them up from his scripts."

Thorne Olson named a major New York publisher. "We sent them tapes of a few of the stories. They were wild about them. Terry's just getting the copy into shape for the typesetters."

"Stories?" Dave sat on the desk corner and picked up the top script. A green-and-blue logo, KPIM, was printed in its upper-left-hand corner. *The Fox Olson Show.* He started to leaf through it. But Thorne came back and took it out of his hands and pushed brandy at him instead. She dropped the script back on the pile.

"Later," she said. "I'll give you some scripts to take with you, if you like. Right now I want you to listen to me, please. We haven't a lot of time." She glanced at her watch. "I'm expecting . . . someone at four." She turned to the girl. "Terry, we'll be in your way. Suppose you take the rest of the day off?"

The girl blinked at her, then gave a little so-what shrug, got up and took from a corner closet a white raincoat. Wasting no time, she put it on while she walked to the door. She threw Dave a small smile, gave Thorne Olson a look that might have meant anything or nothing, then went out and shut the door. They heard her feet go fast and young down the outside stairs.

"Fox spoiled her." Thorne covered the typewriter. "Of course, I'm letting her go. There'll be nothing for her to do once the book is finished. If"—irony was heavy in her voice—"she ever finishes it. Unless I'm out here with her, she spends all her time mooning over Fox's tapes. She adored him, of course."

"I gather a lot of people did," Dave said.

"Thousands." She drew the curtains from a big window that looked down the canyon. The view today was full of muted colors, like a Sung landscape. A couch faced the window—deep, square-built, comfortable-looking. "Shall we sit down?" she said.

Then, "No, wait. First, I want you to look at this room. Carefully. Go ahead."

He did. It was big and nearly square, ceiled and walled with perforated Celotex tile, soundproof, painted eggshell white to set off the pictures. Neat, bright, posterlike, they were signed "Fox Olson," but they were very different from the looming stiff white skeleton thing above the fireplace in the house.

Like the drapes and furniture, the carpeting was mottled autumn reds and yellows. Black cables snaked across it, leading from the elaborate tape-recording equipment to microphones that hung from glittering booms. There were guitars and cases for guitars, a spinet piano piled with music manuscript. T squares, triangles, French curves glinted on an orange square of pegboard above a broad soft pine expanse of drafting table. Sleek, hand-rubbed Danish teak cabinets held art supplies, a hi-fi rig.

He saved the books and records for last. There were lots of them, on handsomely carpentered shelves. The books ran to biographies of American writers. There were novels. Only the best. Not always the popular best but always the knowledgeable best. The records came as a surprise, considering what he'd heard on the Daffodil radio. There was no popular stuff. A lot of Mozart, a lot of the late romantics, Mahler, Bruckner, Sibelius. A lot of opera. But that was forgivable in a singer.

He turned away. "All right." He smiled. "It's a nice lay-out."

Thorne sat watching him from a corner of the

couch, her feet tucked up, an arm in its checked wool sleeve extended along the back of the couch, a cigarette burning in the fingers. She said, "It's everything he ever wanted."

Dave walked toward her, brows raised.

"After a lifetime of wanting," she said. "Let me tell you about this man Fox Olson."

He let himself down on the other end of the couch and lit a cigarette and smoked it and sipped his brandy while she talked.

"He had talent, intelligence, taste, sensitivity. He was good-looking. He had charm and a sense of humor. He could write, paint, sing, play, compose—"

"A thousand and one admirers," Dave said.

"I was the first in line." She smiled, maybe a little bitterly. "He was nineteen when I met him. I was a year younger. It was during the war. The aircraft factories—remember? I'd just graduated from high school. Here in Pima we were . . . out of things. All the excitement. I wanted to be in the middle. I ran away to Los Angeles and found a job. They were hiring anybody and everybody, you know. Lots of women, lots of girls. I riveted P-38s and Hudson bombers for Lockheed. Fox was a timekeeper."

"Why wasn't he in the service?"

Small lines appeared between her brows. She shook her head. "I don't know. He never told me and I didn't ask. I was just thankful. I was in love with him. He was the most romantic creature I could imagine. He was writing. He had a little room at the very top of an old frame house in Hollywood. Franklin Avenue. He'd work graveyard shift and, when he got home in the morning, write. He had an ancient Underwood and he hammered it as if he were beating down doors."

"What?" Dave asked.

"What did he write? Everything. Novels, plays, verse. He ate in drugstores and slept on a sleazy old couch that made down into a bed. He didn't care. Not about anything except writing. He even grew a beard to save the shaving time. He'd show me what he was doing. He was so excited. He'd rip sheets out of the typewriter and toss them at me. We both thought they were wonderful . . ."

With a little remembering smile she sat forward now, elbows on knees, and stared out the big window at the fog and drizzle in the trees.

"Publishers didn't agree. Out went the manuscripts . . . I remember carrying them to the little branch post office down near Hollywood Boulevard on days like this, and trudging home wet to the skin to find the mailbox full of rejected ones." She glanced at him. "It was disappointing, but it was kind of romantic too, an adventure. Then. We were very young." She stopped smiling. "We didn't stay young."

She went to the bar again for the brandy bottle and inched the amber stuff into Dave's glass and her own.

"We had a baby—Gretchen. The war ended. The aircraft factories let people go. We'd thought Fox would be on all the bookshelves in the country by then. Pulitzer Prize, no less. We'd kept thumbing the biographical dictionary to check how young American writers had been when their first books were published." She sighed. "Fox passed all their ages. I hated seeing it. He grew—well, thin. He was sick a lot. He wouldn't let me work before the baby came. Afterward it was out of the question—or so he felt. He was the responsible male. He must do it all, work and write. He took grubby little dollar-an-hour jobs in bookshops. And when he came home he pounded the typewriter. They were always novels now. And a novel takes a long time to write. He got more and more frustrated and bewildered when book after book came back rejected. He was always swearing he'd never touch the typewriter again. But he couldn't stop. Some kind of desperation drove him."

Back of the handsome desk stood a pair of gray steel file cabinets. She led Dave to them, stooped and pulled open a lower drawer. Lined up inside, like the sheeted dead after some disaster, he saw thick manuscripts in binders. She slid one out, stood and turned over the pages. They were, he saw, neatly typed, but the paper had been cheap. It was turning brown at the edges.

"He wrote this one in 1953, 1954. How fine I thought it was." With a small, sad laugh, she closed the covers, bent and pushed the manuscript back into its slot. "It wasn't, I guess. Nobody would publish it." She stood and watched her foot as it rolled the drawer shut. "There are twelve novels in this cabinet. Three plays. Fifty short stories. Hundreds of poems." She looked at Dave and her voice was dry with remembered resentment. "Out of it all, only a handful of poems ever saw print."

Dave frowned. "You're telling me about a failure. What happened?"

3

"To make it a success story?" she asked. "We came to Pima . . . But look, really I haven't told you about him. I've left out too much. For instance, how funny he was. I've only told you about the despair. But he had a marvelous sense of humor." She touched the scripts on the desk. "You'll see when you read these. Antic and zany and never cruel. Just warm and wildly funny."

"And the music," Dave said. "What about that?"

"Yes, that was there too. Not that he ever counted it much. It was"—she gave a little shrug and went back to the couch and sat down and picked up her glass—"a habit. His people were musical. He'd sung and played ever since he was old enough to make a noise. It was in his blood. He took it for granted, like breathing."

Her brown eyes warmed, recalling.

"Sometimes, when the gloom grew gloomiest about the writing, he'd suddenly dust off his guitar and sing all evening. Old songs, songs he made up himself. Friends would come in. We'd drink beer . . . It wasn't all dust and Dostoevsky."

She glanced at him wryly and away again.

"Just mostly. And the good times grew fewer and

19

fewer. We weren't in our twenties anymore. Then we weren't even in our thirties anymore. Gretchen was growing up and needing things girls need. So Fox quit the bookshop and went to work in a factory because the wages were better. And he didn't have the energy he used to have. Naturally, who does? It grew harder and harder for him to write. He kept trying. But he didn't joke much anymore. There were a lot of silences. . . ."

She gazed out the window again, looking her age, looking like someone too much has happened to.

"So you came to Pima," Dave said. "Why?"

"My father had a stroke and sent for me."

"I'm sorry. Is he all right now?"

"He'll never be the same, but he manages. He can walk again. Drive his own car. That was a year ago last summer. It was strange, coming back."

"You hadn't been back at all?" Dave asked.

"Not in twenty-two years. Dad was very angry about my running away. He was even angrier about my marrying Fox. He wrote to tell me so and then he never wrote again, not even when Gretchen was born. You see, he'd planned for me to marry somebody else, a rich boy here in Pima. I didn't want to. Not a very original story, is it?" Her smile was thin, self-mocking. "And I thought, we'll show the old bastard. My husband will be the most successful writer in America. While I was down on my knees scrubbing worn-out linoleum in our grubby little rented kitchens in L.A., I'd dream of the sweet, vengeful day I'd come back to Pima. In glory. Wife of the famous novelist. Small-town girl makes good."

"And thumbs nose at Dad. He's well off, is he?"

"He came to California in 1933, the dust bowl time. From Oklahoma. I was ten. The way he tells it, he arrived"—she said it with a country twang—"'in a five-dollar Ford with my old woman and my sprout here and thirty cents in my pocket.' By 1938 he owned his own ranch free and clear. And in a matter of months after the government ran the Japanese Americans out in 1942, he had one of the largest spreads in this valley. Grapes, citrus, truck. Yes . . . my father's well off. And nobody'd better forget it." She glanced at her watch again. "But we're wasting time. You want to know about Fox. I want to tell you. . . ."

"The success story." Dave nodded.

"It was purest accident." She lifted the bottle at him. He shook his head. She poured herself a finger of brandy and lit another cigarette. "I was at the A&P in Pima, buying supplies for Dad's ranch. And this man stopped me and asked if I wasn't Thorne Loomis. It was Hale McNeil. We'd gone to high school together. Well, not exactly together. He was three years ahead of me. But it's a small school. We knew each other. His father owned the Pima Valley *Sun*. Now Hale owns it—and the radio station.

"Well, it was fun, of course. It always is, meeting someone who used to—you knew as a kid. He was happy about it too, seemingly. And he invited me and Fox and Gretchen to his house for Sunday barbecue. Well, the round with Dad was pretty grim. Oh, there were nurses. But he demanded a lot of attention from me. And Gretchen. And he made no bones about hating Fox's guts. It was being pretty miserable for Fox. He loved the place—the valley, the town, this canyon. But not the situation, understandably. He'd only come because I'd insisted.

"So of course I knew Hale was just being polite when he asked us. He expected to be turned down, probably. But I took him up on his invitation. Just to have something different to do. Someplace to go. Maybe someplace pleasant for a change. Especially for Fox and Gretchen. And we did go. And there were maybe a dozen people. All very nice, the kind of easygoing moneyed people you find in places like Pima. Not many pretensions.

"And one of them, not too surprisingly, had a guitar with him. He hardly knew how to hold it, let alone play it. So naturally Fox began to show him chords or strums or something. And before I knew it, before he knew it himself, he was singing. And people weren't talking anymore. They were standing around listening. And applauding. And was it good for Fox! I hadn't seen him so happy since——" She shrugged. "Well, since Gretchen was toddling around in diapers.

"We ate. Glorious steaks. The sun was setting. And Hale suggested Fox sing some more. Everybody seemed to favor that idea. So he sang some more. And then, just about dark, he leaned back against the barbecue chimney, chording the guitar, and began to tell this absurd small-town story. Well, they laughed till they cried. So did I. It was a total surprise to me. I'd never heard him do such a thing. He said afterward he never had. It was"——she breathed a laugh and tossed her hands up—"just sheer, insane inspiration.

"The next morning Hale phoned the ranch. He asked to talk to Fox. And with Dad listening in on the extension—it never fails—Hale said he'd been thinking over last night, and laughing over it, and what would Fox say to doing a radio program on KPIM. Sing, tell stories, play records. Fox said he wasn't a professional entertainer. Hale said he was professional enough to suit him. Well, Fox had quit the factory to come with me. Had no job. So he said he'd try it. And that's how it began. . . ."

Dave watched her stub out her cigarette. The ashtray was a rough stone mortar. The table was Danish teak.

"Instant success?" he asked.

"It took a while," she said. "Hardly anyone noticed at first. Then suddenly, at the end of maybe six weeks, nobody in Pima, or in the whole valley, for that matter, seemed to be talking about anything else. Yes. It was success, beyond any of our wildest dreams. Money poured in. Every advertiser in the valley wanted to be part of it. There were so many commercials that by Thanksgiving the show had stretched from two hours to four.

"We'd dreamed of a house of our own in a place like this canyon. Sitting huddled there in L.A. with the gas heater going and keeping warm with mugs of instant coffee, we'd plan and plan. Every room. Loving detail. So we were going to build. Luckily, we didn't have to. This place was practically new. The couple who'd built it—the man had gotten a promotion. They had to move East. When we saw it we fell in love with it.

"Especially Fox—with this room. Of course, it was empty then. And it was perfect. Now there was the money. He made his dream come true." She stood and paced the room, looking at it, loving it. The brandy was working. Was she going to get sentimental? He hoped not. He'd begun to like her. "The tape machine, the sound system, the art stuff, the Goya guitar, the Gulbransen piano. All of it exactly the way he wanted. Even the books. Exactly. Do you know they're first editions? Most of them signed." She took a book down, opened the cover. "William Carlos Williams . . ."

"I noticed," Dave said.

She put the book back and touched the shiny metal of the tall stands. "These microphones cost three hundred dollars each. They're the finest made."

"What about the painting?" Dave asked. "Where did that come in?"

"The painting?" She opened blank eyes at him. The brandy had worked. "Oh . . . I thought I told you. Before the war, Pearl Harbor, he studied art. For a year, at the Provence School. On Western Avenue. He and a friend, Doug Sawyer. I never knew him. He joined the Air Force. Lost on a bombing mission over Europe in the first months. That was when Fox went into the aircraft factory.

"He told me when we met that he'd never touch a brush again. And it was a good many years before he wanted to. And then there wasn't time or strength.

Not with working eight hours a day and writing too. And he'd invested too much in the writing to stop that. Years. So painting was one of those things he was going to do when his book got published and became a best seller and we were rich."

"And you got rich and he started. Right?"

"Right." She finished the last of her brandy and set the glass down with a click. "And the book is going to be a reality too. All those years of writing are going to pay off at last. Do you know what the advance royalty was? Twenty-five thousand dollars. That, my friend, is success! He was illustrating it himself. Here . . ." She slid a portfolio from the art cabinet and opened it on the drafting table. Dave went to look. The drawings were ink and wash. Quick and funny and filled with small-town atmosphere.

"I'll have to read the stories," he said.

"You do that." The brandy hadn't softened her. It had dissolved the polish. She walked to the desk, scooped up the heap of scripts, came back and thrust them into his hands. "And try to forget your grade-B-thriller theories, Mr. Brandstetter. Fox Olson didn't demolish his new six-thousand-dollar car and trudge off into nowhere in the middle of a rainy night. He'd reached the best years of his life. They were just beginning. Record companies were interested. Television . . ." She glanced at her watch again. "See Hale McNeil, if you still have any doubts. At KPIM. He'll show you the letters, the contract offers. Now I'm sorry, but you're going to have to excuse me. . . ."

Dave smiled. "There'll be other days."

"I hope not!" she flared. "Frankly, I'm really quite upset and angry about this. It's perfectly senseless. When the storm is over, Fox's body will be found. Then you'll feel as absurd as I know right now you are." She turned away. "Come along. I'll give you your coat. . . ."

When he reached his car, under the dripping, blue-gray manzanita, his feet wet again from the shallow river that was the road, he tossed the damp scripts into the back seat. He started the engine, released the brake. But he wasn't leaving yet. He drove up the road fifty yards, argued the car around, twice nearly sinking the rear wheels in a pothole big enough to qualify as a scenic wonder, and parked with the engine running. There was a lot of wet green brush here. Mountain holly. It masked the car.

He waited. About five minutes. Then a station wagon swung into the Olson driveway. Green-and-blue logo on the door: KPIM. Dave slid across the seat. The blurred glass didn't help, but through a gap in the brush he saw the station wagon brake behind the Mustang. The old Chevy was gone. It must have belonged to the girl, Terry.

The driver got out of the station wagon. Distance and rain made it impossible to see his features. He was well set up, broad in the shoulders. No hat. Dark hair. Tan fly-front coat. Head down, he trotted along the flags toward the house. Dave lost sight of him in the tangle of brush for a second. Then he found a gap that showed him the house door. It opened.

Fadeout

Thorne Olson came out, still in the brown boy's clothes. She ran five steps through the rain and into the man's arms. He closed them around her. She clung to him and he bent his head and covered her mouth with a kiss. They stood there locked together for a good fifteen seconds. More than enough time for a polite exchange of greetings. Then they went into the house and the door closed.

Dave waited a few minutes, then let the hand brake go and headed back down the canyon.

4

She was rolling a wheel along the road. When the
tire wobbled against her it smeared mud on
the white raincoat. She had tied a triangle of clear
plastic over her hair. It lay like drenched tissue paper.
When she heard the car come up behind her and
turned to look at him, strands of wet hair lay plastered down her face. She raked at them with the
fingers of one muddy hand and gave him a little
frantic wave with the other. The wheel got away
from her then. It lurched into the roadside scrub
and lay down like a sick animal.

He set the hand brake and got out. The water
thundered down the arroyo. Over its roar, he
shouted, "Get into the car."

"The wheel!" she wailed.

"I'll bring it," he said. "Get in."

When he opened the luggage compartment the
smell of new automobile came out. He'd only opened
it twice. For suitcases. Well, all that handsome,
contoured carpeting was due for a shock. He heaved
the split and earth-clogged tire inside and slammed
the lid. Now his own coat was muddy. He sighed,
wiped his hands on it and climbed back into the
car behind the steering wheel.

"Gosh, thanks." She perched, dripping, on the seat edge. "But I'm ruining your lovely new car."

"It's a company car," he said. "They expect me to use it hard. Like James Bond."

"What company? Who are you? Brand what?"

"Brandstetter, David. Medallion Life. I'm an insurance investigator." He let go the hand brake and began to inch the car along again. The rain came down hard now. The windshield wipers waved like the arms of a drowning man. "What did you think you were doing?"

"I had a flat and no spare. I was walking to Pima. My boyfriend works at the Signal station." She looked at her muddy hands. "Have you got a Kleenex or something?"

Keeping watch on the road, what he could see of it, he leaned across and opened the glove compartment. There was a box of tissues. Blue box with little white tracery flowers. He jerked some of the soft papers out and handed them to her. "How come you didn't go back to Olson's?"

She sneezed. A plastic bag for trash hung off the dashboard. Thoughtful Medallion. She stuffed the muddied Kleenex into it and pulled fresh ones to blow her nose. "They don't have a spare."

"I meant, you could have phoned from there."

"*He's* there," she said.

Dave glanced at her. "When did you get this flat? You left up there a good hour ago. Where's your car?"

"Back up the road. A little below the bridge."

"I didn't see it," Dave said.

"It's parked up that little overgrown side road that used to lead to a house that burned down."

"What were you doing there?"

"Waiting." Her face set. Young, sullen. She muttered, "There was something I wanted to see."

"Who was coming to Olson's—right?"

"Right. It was him. Hale McNeil. When you didn't come down, I began to wonder if it would be. But it was. Him. He. Then, when I started up my car, the damn tire was flat. My third in two weeks . . . Can I have a cigarette, please? I left mine in my car."

He dug out his pack and handed it to her. "There's a dash lighter," he said. "It sounds to me as if you either ought to get new tires or stop backing up country roads to spy on your employer. Why shouldn't Hale McNeil visit Mrs. Olson? They're old friends."

The smoke from the cigarette hung gray and still in the warm car. She blinked at him through it. "Insurance investigators come around when there's something wrong," she said. "You think there's something wrong about Fox Olson's death, don't you?"

He watched the road. "Do you?"

"Yes." She poked the lighter back into its socket. "I think he committed suicide."

"Why?" The smoke smelled good. "Light one of those for me, would you?"

"Because Thorne and Hale are having an affair." She pushed the lighter and hung the new cigarette in her mouth. All the lipstick was gone. It looked vulnerable as a flower.

"You think," he asked, "or you know?"

"I know." She lit the cigarette and leaned across and set it carefully in his mouth. "I saw them. Last July. Right out in broad daylight. Naked. By the pool. Disgusting. I mean, how revolting can you get? They're old enough to be grandparents or something." She thrust the lighter back into place.

He grinned. "I have news. We senior citizens have our moments. Thank God." He glanced at her. "Anyway, I assume they thought they were alone."

"I wasn't supposed to be there," she admitted. "It was my day off. But Sandy and I—Sandy Webb, the one who works at the gas station—we'd had a fight. I didn't feel like sitting around moping . . . Where's the ashtray?"

"Reach under the dash," he said. "It tilts out."

She found it and tilted it out and put ashes into it.

"So I thought I'd go up to the studio and work. I didn't get far. They didn't see me. I cut out. I was sick. I drove straight to the station—KPIM. Fox was taping two shows that day. He did that on Wednesdays. It was why I had the day off. Maria too. She cooks and keeps house. That was why Thorne and Hale—"

"Today's Monday," Dave said. "I didn't see Maria."

"She moved out when Fox died. She doesn't like Thorne. It was Fox she liked." Her smile was crooked and forlorn. "Everybody liked Fox."

"Was Thorne hard to work for?"

31

"It wasn't that. She fired Maria. Last Christmas. Well, you just don't do that to Maria."

"What was the reason?"

"Thorne hired a Japanese houseboy. Through an agency in San Francisco. A Christmas gift to Fox. She said when they were poor back in L.A. and daydreamed about getting successful and having servants, Fox always said a Japanese houseboy was the only kind he'd want. You know?"

"So what happened to the houseboy?"

"Oh, he's still in town. Works at the Pima Motor Inn."

"I didn't mean that. I meant, why was it he didn't last?"

"I don't know exactly. . . ." She frowned and stubbed out her cigarette. "I remember, the day after Christmas, he was out in a pair of little white trunks, vacuuming the pool. About nine in the morning. When I walked into the studio Fox was standing by the window. He didn't hear me, didn't see me, just stood there staring down at Ito for the longest time. Then, suddenly, he turned and without a word ran out of the studio and down the stairs and into the house. Pretty soon Thorne came out and called Ito inside. After that, Fox came back up. But he was very quiet all day . . . Ito was never around the place after that."

"And Maria came back?"

The girl nodded. "But not speaking to Thorne. Not for quite a while."

The rain had brought night early. He switched on the headlights. "I interrupted you," he said. "You

were telling me about what you did after you found
Mr. McNeil and Mrs. Olson making out beside the
pool."

"I drove straight to the station to tell Fox. But
when I ran inside and saw him through the studio
window, sitting there at the long table with those
big, white pillow earphones on, and the mike
hanging in front of his face, and the scripts and the
music and record sleeves and empty paper cups,
with his guitar in his hands, grinning and being
funny for the people . . ."

She bit her lip and turned away to face the darkness. She couldn't go on for a minute. When she
did, when she turned toward him and he glanced
at her, her face was wet as if there hadn't been glass
between it and the rain.

"He was so sweet. Such a dear, kind, gentle guy.
I couldn't. I couldn't bear to hurt him." She reached
for the Kleenex again.

Dave said, "But he committed suicide anyway?"

"He found out. Himself. He must have. It was
Wednesday night when he died. I don't know. I
wasn't there. But I bet he came home when she
didn't expect him. And found them the way I did
before."

"Not by the pool," Dave said. "Not in this
weather."

She cried, "Stop laughing. It's not funny. It's
tragic! I know him. I know how he would have felt.
He wouldn't even tell them."

Dave raised his eyebrows. "Hated scenes, did he?"

"Oh, stop," she said. "No. You don't understand

him at all." She turned away sharply. "You probably won't believe it, but how he'd react would be: 'I don't want to spoil their happiness.'"

"If you say so," Dave said. "I didn't know him."

"He turned around and drove back down the canyon and crashed through that bridge. Killed himself."

"He loved her that much?"

"What do you mean? She was his wife."

Dave smiled without cheer. "Had been for twenty-odd years. You've hardly lived that long. You don't know how long that can be." He put out his cigarette.

"He wouldn't look at another woman," she said hotly. "Everything he did was for her."

"I see." Dave nodded ahead. "Here's Pima." Through the rain it was a huddled smear of neon reds and blues. "You'll have to direct me. Where's this Signal station?"

She pointed. "Turn right at the traffic light. Gee, I'm grateful, Mr. Brand—what?"

"Stetter," he told her again.

He drove under the gas-station overhang. Sheet metal. The rain rattled on it. A boy came out of the bright glass office. Black slicker open over his tan uniform. Tall, with a child's face under a mop of reddish hair.

"It's me, Sandy." Terry got out of the car. "I had another flat."

He didn't answer, only stared at her.

"Mr. Brandstetter gave me a ride. The wheel's in his trunk."

Dave leaned across the seat and held out keys.

The boy took them with a big hand, grease under the nails. Turning, he said to the girl, "Shit."

Dave got out. The boy had the back open.

"What's your problem?" Dave said.

The boy bounced the wheel. It splashed water and mud off the tarmac. He shut the trunk and handed Dave his keys. "No problem," he said. "I'll fix it for her."

"You're very gallant," Dave said.

"Am I supposed to thank you for picking up my chick?"

"It was my pleasure." Dave smiled at the girl.

"I'll bet it was," the boy sneered. "Christ . . ." He turned on the girl. "What is it with you and dirty old men?"

His shirt was open at the handsome throat. Dave started to reach for it. Terry caught his arm.

"No, don't," she said. "He didn't mean it. Sandy, why do you act like this?"

The boy didn't answer. He glowered.

Dave took Terry's elbow. "Come on. You'd better let me drive you home."

"Like hell," the boy said.

"It's all right, Mr. Brandstetter. He won't hurt me. He's just jealous, is all that's wrong with him." She eyed the boy with loving scorn. "Not quite an adult yet."

"Shit!" The boy rolled the tire toward the garage.

Dave folded himself back into his car. "Advise him," he said to Terry, "that I don't sing, play the guitar, tell stories or paint pictures. And that I have practically no sense of humor."

She blinked wide blue eyes at him.

"See you later," he said and let the car door click shut and tilted the car out into the street. Broad, high-curbed, empty in the rain. The yellow store windows looked bleak. Against the murky dusk, the gaudy signs spelled loneliness.

5

Phil Mundy looked at Dave through a bright aluminum screen door that was the only new thing about the shack. Shack was the word. Part bat and board, part tar paper and chicken wire, it squatted in the middle of five weedy acres of dying fruit trees and abandoned chicken coops on the outskirts of Pima. Near the tracks.

Waiting, muddy-footed, on the sagging wooden stoop, with the night rain leaking cold down the back of his neck, Dave realized that Mundy looked like Fox Olson, the photo in Medallion's files, the photo distributed now to police departments across the country. Even to the thinning blond hair. Except that Olson had a good mouth. Mundy's there was something wrong with. A little too small, a little too tight.

"Who is it, Phil?" A woman's voice, raucous, the speech slurred. She stood back inside the room, squinting. Not old. Not more than forty-five. But badly worn. Uncombed dyed blond hair. Soiled flower-print kimono. In her puffy hand a glass of oily-looking yellow liquid.

"It's the man from the insurance company," Phil said without turning. He worked the latch, pushed the screen. "Come in, Mr. Brandstetter. Gretchen will be right back."

Dave stepped inside.

"I'm running out of vino," the woman giggled at him. Bad teeth. She was trying to flirt. Not trying. It was a reflex. "Gretchen's gone to get me 'nother fifth." Her mouth was poorly painted. She twisted it into a smile that lied. "She always gets me anything I want."

"This is my mother," Mundy said. He shut the front door. It was swollen with damp. He had to shoulder it. "Mom, why don't you go see if Buddy needs anything?"

"He's all right," she said. "I just gave him his bath. He's watching the TV."

"Well, why don't you go watch it with him?" Mundy had a gentle, patient voice. He was very young but he acted as if he'd managed her forever.

Her eyes were big, heavy-lidded, slightly protuberant. They rolled at him sullenly. "Pushed around in my own house," she grumbled. But she left, remembering to sway her hips even though it made her stagger.

"Let me take your coat," Mundy said. "I'm sorry Mom's like this tonight." His smile was feeble. "She's not . . . always. We try to keep her from getting it, but—"

"Don't apologize for her," Dave said.

Phil winced and his voice went adolescent. "I'm not. I wouldn't do that. I just want you to understand . . ."

"I understand." Dave made his voice kind.

38

"Thanks . . . Well, look, why don't you sit down?" Mundy took the coat away.

Dave sat. Somebody had worked hard to make the room cheerful. New cottagey wallpaper. Creamy new paint on the woodwork. Chintz curtains to match the new slipcovers on the lumpy old furniture. The warped floorboards painted and waxed. Throw rugs braided out of bright rags. Fox Olson still lifes on the walls—golden squashes, green peppers, tomatoes. Somebody had worked hard, but too much hopelessness and defeat had shaped the room. It wouldn't smile.

Phil came back and stood with his hands in his pockets. "Gretchen didn't go after wine," he said. "She wanted to offer you a drink. We'd like one ourselves. But we can't keep it around."

"I understand," Dave said.

"It's awkward, but the only time to buy it is just before the guest arrives."

"It's very kind," Dave said.

There was a splash of tires in the muddy yard, steps on the porch, the shudder of the wet front door. Gretchen came in, untying a transparent rain cape, giving it a noisy shake. She slid the bottle out of its damp brown paper sack and set it on the telephone stand. "Hello!" She smiled, crumpling the sack. "I'll be back in a minim. I hope you like rye."

"Fine." She was damn cheerful for a new orphan. She came back with glasses, ice in a bowl, a pitcher of water. She was small like her mother, and had her mother's brown hair and eyes. She even wore brown like her mother, brown turtleneck sweater, cable-knit, bulky on her slightness, brown tweed miniskirt, brown tights. But the personality wasn't Thorne's any more than were the bright orange earrings and loops of crazy beads. This had to be the famous Fox Olson charm.

"No fit night," she said, sitting on the couch edge, dropping ice cubes into glasses, "for woman nor beast. Nor, I should think, insurance investigator. What brings you through storm and sleet, Mr. B.?"

He didn't smile. He asked, "Do you miss your father?"

She paused with the jigger in one hand and the flat pint bottle of Old Overholt in the other. Her face sobered. She looked straight at him. "I'm going to miss him every minute of every day for the rest of my life," she said. "If I weren't my mother's daughter, I'd be crying my eyes out right now, I promise you. But Thorne doesn't cry, doesn't know how. And neither do I. I wish I did." She watched him gravely for a few more seconds, then the smile came back and she went on fixing the drinks. She handed him the first.

"Thank you," he said. "Do you think he's dead?"

Phil Mundy fumbled the glass his wife was handing him and dropped it. His face was the color of putty.

"Oh, Phil, darling!" Gretchen cried. "I'm sorry."

"No, no." Phil was down on his knees after the glass and ice. "My fault. Clumsy." He stood up. "I'll . . . get a rag, wipe it up." He ran out.

"What did you say?" Gretchen frowned, two little upright lines between her brows, like her mother.

"I asked if you think your father is dead."

"Don't you?" Blank bewilderment. "Isn't he?"

"His body can't be found. That's the reason my company sent me here. To learn why."

"Why what?" She gave a little laugh but she was troubled. "What do you mean, why?"

"Why almost anything." Dave shrugged. "Why, for example, would he want to make it look as if he were dead?"

"Well, I—" She shook her head impatiently. "No, he wouldn't. I mean—what for? He was busy and happy and successful. That was why I felt free to marry Phil. Fox didn't need me anymore."

Phil came back with a damp cloth and sopped up the spilled whiskey. "You trying to say Mr. Olson isn't dead?"

"Captain Herrera, the sheriff's office, the forestry department tell me the body should have been found Friday in the arroyo," Dave said. "It wasn't. It looks as if, for some reason, he disappeared."

"Ridiculous." Phil stood up, both hands cradling the wet rag to keep it from dripping. "I mean, excuse me. I don't mean to be rude. But he's got to be dead. Sure. After the storm's over, they'll find him down the river somewhere . . . Look, I'll be back." He carried off the rag.

"You said your father didn't need you anymore," Dave said to Gretchen. "What does that mean?"

She looked away and gave a little shrug. "His life was full now. I mean, twenty-five hours a day. There weren't any sad, empty times. When he and Thorne sat and blamed each other."

41

"They fought?"

Her brown eyes reproached him. "They're a little fine for that, don't you think?"

He said, "I never met your father. I saw your mother this afternoon, only for a couple of hours."

She said, "No, it wasn't spoken. It was silent. And terrible. She was so sorry for him. She was so angry at the world that wouldn't pay any attention to him. So angry at him because he'd stopped believing in himself. He was going through the motions anymore just to . . . please her, show her he hadn't given up. But he'd given up. And she knew it. And that made it all the more terrible. The silences . . ."

"So you"—Dave smiled—"broke up the silences?"

"Whenever I could. He and I are a lot alike. Were. We'd kid around. Funny voices, vaudeville accents, German, Japanese, hicks. The bits, you know. And sing. He taught me to sing before I could walk. And the guitar, naturally, as soon as I could hold one." He had noticed it standing in the corner. "Toward the end in L.A., he'd never sing anymore unless I'd start and sucker him into showing me chords, teaching me the words of songs—something like that."

Dave shifted in the butt-sprung chair. "Your mother doesn't like music much, does she?"

Gretchen looked at him sideways. "What makes you say that?"

"There's no sound system in the house. It's all out in your father's studio. No records. No musical instruments . . ."

42

"You're right." She smiled. "You should be an insurance investigator."

"I may take it up," he said. "Was he a good writer?"

She frowned into her glass. "Yes . . . in a sense. A good craftsman. I mean, inevitably. He'd read everything. He'd written millions of words. He was intelligent. He had taste." She chewed her lip, doubting. "He was a . . . good writer. But something was missing. I don't know what. Something, though. It was always as if he was talking about the wrong thing."

"How?" Dave tilted his glass up for a last swallow.

"Not what was really on his mind." She shook her head, with a little puzzled smile. "As if there was something else he ought to be talking about instead. Is that clear?"

He grinned and lifted his glass at her. "That was very good. And it was very good of you to drive off through the rain to fetch it for me."

She laughed. "Okay, so I'm not a literary critic . . . As to Old Overshoe—I might have offered you coffee. But that's so dispiriting when you're dying for booze." She held out her hand. "Let me fix you another."

He gave her the glass. "Was your father drinking a lot?"

Hands busy, she glanced at him. "Well . . . yes, I suppose so. The expensive people in Pima Valley do drink a lot. Like the rural rich everywhere in the West, I gather. Fox and Thorne were running with a merry group. And he was working hard. It helped him relax." She handed Dave the fresh drink. "But he certainly wasn't an alcoholic."

"Not drowning his sorrows?"

"He hadn't any sorrows," she said. "Not anymore."

"This book of his stories—was he happy about it?"

"Very." She nodded.

"Was that what he'd always written—humor?"

"Far from it," she said. "Gloom and doom. Lots of pain and death and failure. Dust and cobwebs."

"So maybe comedy was what he ought to have been doing all along," Dave said. "Could that be what you meant by his writing about . . . the wrong things."

"Looks that way," she said.

Phil stood in the doorway. "Mr. Brandstetter, it's my brother's bedtime. And he'd like to meet you. He hates to miss anybody. See . . . he can't get out much." The blue eyes pleaded.

Dave glanced at Gretchen. She looked hopeful. He set down his drink and stood up smiling. "Lead the way."

The room was at the back of the ramshackle house. It had been painted and papered with the same love as the front room, only here the love had paid off, maybe just because of the room's occupant. There were shelves stacked with tattered *National Geographics* and paperback books frayed from reading. Model cars stood on the dresser. The ceiling was covered with automobile license plates. A worktable was littered with tiny bottles of bright plastic paint and glue. There was an old electric typewriter, a new television set. A scarred white hospital bed dominated the room. Beside it, in a wheelchair, sat a boy.

His body was ten-year-old size, in fresh blue cotton pajamas and a plaid bathrobe. His head with its wetly combed-down hair was too big for his body. It was a handsome head but hard for him to control. It rolled back and to the side when he saw Dave. The mouth stretched, trying for a smile and for words. In time he managed both. The words came haltingly and loud. It was almost a man's voice.

"Thank you . . . for com . . . ing back," he said.

It wasn't easy for him to make his hand go where he wanted it to. It strayed from his lap, the arm bending too much and too often at the elbow and the wrist, the fingers curling and stiffening. But finally he had it out for a handshake. Dave took it. The grip was warm and convulsively strong.

"It's good to meet you, Buddy," he said. "This is quite a room you've got here." He looked at the models again. "These are beautiful." He nudged a 1932 Ford along the dresser top.

"They help me . . . learn . . . coordination," Buddy said.

Dave looked at him for a second without understanding. He had thought Phil or Gretchen must have put them together. Christ, the agonizing patience of the kid!

"Do you . . . play chess, Mr. . . . Brand . . . stetter?"

"I'm what's called a potzer." Dave grinned.

The boy laughed. It was a loud, strangling sound. "Have you got . . . time for a . . . game?"

"Oh, Buddy," Gretchen protested, "it's after nine, sweetheart. You know you need your rest."

"Anyway . . ." Phil was standing beside the wheelchair. He drew the boy's head affectionately against him. "Mr. Brandstetter's only here on business for his company."

Dave looked at the board with the chessmen painstakingly set out. He tried to read in Buddy's eyes, which were gray like the rain, and the only thing not moving in his beautiful, tormented face, how important it was. He decided it was important. He said:

"I'll come back. How about tomorrow afternoon?"

Buddy's head yawed again in an unmeant parody of ecstasy. His mouth worked once more at the smile and the words. "If you don't . . . mind . . . playing another . . . potzer." Hoarse shout of indragged laughter. Happy, crooked wave of the hand.

"I'll be here at four," Dave said.

He had left his car under a walnut tree beside the house. The rain had brought down the tree's tattered, blackened leaves, plastered the hood and roof with them. He cleared them off the windshield, got into the car and started the engine. Then he turned on the headlights and saw Mrs. Mundy. Her kimono was soaked and clung to her loose breasts and belly and hips. She reeled toward him, waving an empty wine bottle.

"Wait!" she bawled. "Hold on, there."

He got out of the car. "Mrs. Mundy, you shouldn't be out in the rain like this. Where's your coat?"

46

"Listen." She clutched his sleeve. Her large, unfocused eyes—maybe they'd once been beautiful—peered up at him through draggled strands of hair. Her breath stank of rotten grapes. "I know what you're here for. You're tryin' to figure out how . . . how your comp'ny won't have to . . . pay us our money."

"Gretchen's money," he said.

"Ours." She nodded. "Fifty—fifty thous'n' dollars. Your comp'ny don't want to pay it, so you're makin' out like Fox Olson never died. Well, I say . . . what if he didn't die? What if he did just . . . dis'pear? So what? What skin is that off your nose, Mr. Brans . . ." She couldn't make her mouth finish it. "Do you know . . .?" she began fiercely, and flung her arm out toward the shack. The bottle flew from her hand. It lit with a wet sound in the darkness. "Do you know what that money can mean to us? To my boys and me? Not her. Her Grandpa's got all the money in the world. But us! Poor Buddy, poor Phil?" The wine had loosened her face. Now self-pity broke it apart. She began to cry. "Be fair, Mr. Brans . . . Have heart. If your comp'ny pays . . . it don't cost you nothin'. It's a tough life. What do you wanna go makin' it tougher for. . . ."

"Come on," he said. He put an arm around her soft, sodden shapelessness and steered her, sobbing, back to the shack.

47

6

The Pima Motor Inn imitated a mission. Cloisters. Thick whitewashed walls. Strings of painted gourds beside the doors. Black iron latches and hinges. Black iron grillwork on the deep-set windows. Worn Indian rugs on the cracked tile floors. Now, after ten days of rain, the place was so damp the walls felt soft. Moss grew in the shower.

He didn't care. Toweling himself—Christ, he'd lost weight these last weeks!—he knew all that mattered was that the place wasn't his, his and Rod's. Madge Dunstan had been right. He ought to have left the house, sold it. It had been a bad place for him to stay from the moment he'd learned Rod was never coming back to it alive. Empty. Worse—haunted.

Because the emptiness hurt, but not so much as the regret. In that wide white wickerwork bed of theirs, regret took the place of sleeping, and at the table in the brick-and-copper kitchen, the place of eating. It made him refuse to pick up the phone, unable to pick up the phone, unable, if he had picked it up, to talk. Even less able to talk to anyone—even Madge—face to face. Regret. Because, as he had told the girl in the car this afternoon, twenty years was a long time.

Fadeout

In twenty years you could say and do a lot you wish you hadn't. In twenty years you could store up a lot of regrets. And then, when it was too late, when there was no one left to say "I'm sorry" to, "I didn't mean it" to, you could stop sleeping for regret, stop eating, talking, working, for regret. You could stop wanting to live. You could want to die for regret.

It was only remembering the good times that kept you from taking the knife from the kitchen drawer and, holding it so, tightly in your fist, on the bed, naked to no purpose except that that was how you came into the world and how your best moments in the world had been spent—holding it so, roll onto the blade, slowly, so that it slid like love between your ribs and into that stupidly pumping muscle in your chest that kept you regretting.

The good memories stopped you.

For him they began with that crazy bed. Nineteen forty-five. He was just out of the army. Los Angeles was crowded. Unable to find an apartment, unwilling to stay with his father and stepmother number four—his own age, pretty and stupid—he had taken the college money banked for him as a kid, and made a down payment on a house. A little old one-story wooden side-street place. Christmas was two weeks off. He wanted to move in before that. Maybe because he was very young, the first thing he thought of buying was a bed.

The nearest furniture store was on Western Avenue, a broad, bright acre of shiny woods and metal-shot fabrics. Tinsel and bells overhead.

Loudspeakers tinkling carols. Crowds of shoppers in rain-damp coats. He edged among them, looking for a clerk. They were all busy. But in a far corner he saw one, a short, dark boy, finishing a sale. The boy took crumpled bills from a worried-looking Mexican woman, punched the cash register, handed the woman her change, and her receipt, and gave her a smile. Dazzling.

I want you, Dave thought, and wondered if he'd said it aloud, because the boy looked at him then, over the heads of a lot of other people. Straight at him. And there was recognition in the eyes, curious opaque eyes, like bright stones in a stream bed. He ignored the other customers. He came to Dave.

"May I help you?" Zero for originality.

"I'm looking for a bed."

For a second, the start of a smile twitched the boy's mouth. It didn't develop. "Single or double?"

"Double," Dave said. "I don't want to sleep alone forever."

The boy didn't react. He was already moving off. "I've got something to show you."

It turned out to be extra wide.

Dave laughed. "I didn't say I wanted to sleep with an army. I hope that's over with."

"Wait," the boy said, "let me tell you about this bed. See, most of the furniture in this place is put together with wooden pegs and glue. Wartime restrictions. But this bed is built. It's prewar. The mattress too. They've been here years. I can give you a good price."

It was white wicker, swirls, arabesques.

"I'll feel like I'm waking up every morning in my bassinet," he said.

The boy let the smile develop now. "Not if you've got somebody with you."

"Seriously, isn't it a little chichi for a male?"

The boy shook his head. "Use rough fabrics for the spread and curtains. Plain colors."

"Will you help me pick them out?"

"Aw . . . I'm sorry." He meant it. "That's in another department."

Dave felt lost. The boy saw it and laughed.

"Don't look so worried. . . ." He began writing out the sales slip. "You can do it. Just stay away from yellow, with your coloring. Blues would be right for you, but too cold with white. Try burnt orange." He looked up. "Name? Address?"

They painted the walls burnt orange, had a spread made to match and curtains of white muslin. Because the boy did help him pick out the fabrics. And the paint. Not for the bedroom only. For the rest of the place too. And to remodel it, something Dave wouldn't have thought of. It was a shambles on Christmas Eve, the floor strewn with tatters of old wallpaper, rumpled tarpaulins, color-dribbled paint cans, buckets of plaster, brushes, putty knives, crowbars . . . He didn't care. He couldn't have been happier.

When he'd seen Rod first, talked to him first, heart running quick as a watch, mouth dry, he had told himself, *This will be good for exactly one sweet night.* The kid was feminine. A flit. Nobody he could live with. A decorator, for Christ sake! One cut above a hairdresser . . . But Christmas Eve, lying naked and warm against Rod in that preposterous bed, both of them with the smell of paint in their hair that no amount of showering would take out, listening to the church bells off across the rainy midnight city, he understood he had been wrong. No, it hadn't gone on long yet. Only two weeks. But he knew, they both knew it was forever. . . .

Now, sitting lonely in the limp and faded blue corduroy bathrobe Rod had given him a dozen birthdays ago, sitting smoking a cigarette on the edge of one of the supersoft twin beds in the damp white room of the Pima Motor Inn, he reflected wryly that what they'd both been too young to know was the meaning of forever. It was what he'd tried to tell the girl in the car today.

How two people could wear on each other. In small ways. Little kid habits like Rod's of leaving things, clothes he'd taken off, magazines he'd read, pans he'd cooked in, right where he'd dropped them. Of "forgetting" chores, the dirty dishes, the greasy stove, when it was his turn to do them. The look of wide-eyed hurt when Dave lost his temper and bawled him out. As if, he thought now, they'd meant anything, done or undone.

Rod had adored the loud, shiny, successful Broadway musicals. In record shops, while Dave sweated out a choice between Messiaen's new *Chronochromie* and an E. Power Biggs Buxtehude organ recital, sure they couldn't afford either, Rod, with cries of glee, would gather armloads of glittering original-cast albums. And play them, morning, noon and night, until Dave threatened to smash them over his head. For every recital of Schönberg songs or Gesualdo madrigals Dave took him to, Rod dragged Dave to half a dozen brassy *Pajama Games, Gypsys, Most Happy Fellas*, where Dave sat in the dark with clenched teeth, groaning for the end. Rod's taste in films had been even worse. He'd worshiped a dim galaxy of minor screen queens, would sit up half the night in the blue glow of the television set enchanted by the tired wisecracks of Iris Adrian or Marie Windsor in forgotten RKO second features of the thirties. . . .

The cigarette was burning his fingers. He mashed it out in the ashtray and sighed grimly. He was thinking wrong again. Regretting again. Sorry for his sourness at Rod's harmless games. Actually, he'd had fun out of them too because happiness with Rod splashed over. Less easy to understand was why Rod had put up with him. He had, after all, sat cheerfully through chamber music recitals Dave knew bored him, trudged amiably at Dave's heels through long galleries of paintings and sculptures that meant nothing to him, listened while Dave read aloud articles on science and war and politics he didn't grasp a tenth of, breathed quietly but awake through hours of static avant-garde films and ancient flickering Dreyer and Griffith classics, with never a murmur of protest. Murmur of protest, hell! With thanks, and with at least a try at talking about them sensibly.

And how good he'd been about his friends. The ones Dave had scattered. Because Rod's taste in people was appalling. Dave didn't need a second evening with any of them to know he couldn't stand it. The giddy mannerisms, the worn-out camp clichés that passed for wit, the shrill, empty chatter about women's clothes and Judy Garland. Not to mention the whimpering two-in-the-morning phone calls from Lincoln Heights jail for rescue from the detectives they'd made passes at. When Dave had slammed the door on some and hung up the phone on the rest, Rod had told him with a wan smile:

"They think you're an ogre."

"I am," Dave said. "I eat boys. But very selectively. Come here. Let me show you."

So there had been mostly only the two of them. It had been enough. After all, the musicals hadn't all been bad, nor the recitals all boring, and the Yvonne de Carlo costumes *were* funny, and Rod's eyes had shone at the glitter of gold and jewels in the "Art Treasures of Ancient Turkey" exhibit, and all the reading hadn't been sternly informational. They'd liked sharing detective stories—Arthur Crook, Nero Wolfe, Miss Marple, characters he wouldn't read about again because they wouldn't speak the same without Rod's voice. He read well. If he hadn't been so nelly he'd have made a fine actor. But it hadn't been possible to school out of him all the femininity. Dave had tried. So had Rod. The affectations went, but what underlay them was ingrained. Real. Himself. Dave gave up trying after a while. Age took care of it to some extent. Death took care of it completely.

No. That was how he mustn't think. Tears came

hot into his eyes. He got up and walked the room. Remember something else. For God's sake, forget about the dying. Remember the trip to Oak Canyon, the cabin in the woods, making love by the light of crackling pine logs, waking in the morning to see out the window the whole landscape snow-muffled, white, white . . . The glinting crystal chandeliers and mirrors of the Music Center. Nureyev leaping in a shaft of golden light . . . The glow of pride when Rod was able to open that first small shop of his, the chaste black-and-gold sign above the white fanlit door: R. FLEMING, INTERIORS . . . The sun-bright Easter morning they'd wakened to find that Tatiana, their fat, striped, indignant old cat (Rod called her Tatty Anna) had presented them with six striped kittens at the foot of the bed . . . The turning, twinkling, tremendous Christmas tree in that Greek Theatre production of *The Nutcracker* one warm, midsummer night . . . Rod's shout of triumphant laughter at the news that he'd been chosen to decorate all the apartments of a new building towering among the fountains of Century City . . . The bulging eyes of the supermarket cashier when he saw the shopping cart full of champagne and oysters, caviar and pâté they'd bought the day the first fantastic check arrived . . . Remember those things. . . .

But he kept remembering instead the eerily whispering corridors of the hospital late that last night, the smells of the hospital, kept seeing sharp and photographic his own feet in their scuffed brown loafers, pacing up and down, up and down, hour after hour, outside the door of the room where Rod's cut and gutted body lay mindless with drugs but still feeding, feeding the spreading, burgeoning red horror that would not die until it killed the thing it fed on. . . .

And he knew he'd never sleep tonight. He got the pint of Old Crow from his suitcase, poured steeply from it into the clear plastic bathroom glass, added a twist of tap water, then took from the dresser top Fox Olson's scripts, and got into bed. Not soon, but sooner than he would have thought, he began to laugh.

7

He even slept. Knocking woke him. He still sat propped against thin pillows and a hard headboard. His neck and shoulders ached. The scripts had slid off his knees. Now, when he straightened his stiff legs under the thin, machine-made Indian-style blankets, the scripts slithered to the floor. The lamp glowed sickly in the daylight. Wincing, he switched it off. In the glass that wasn't glass the dregs of whiskey lurked like a neglected friendship. He made a sound, cleared his throat, tried again.

"Who is it?"

"Coffee, Mr. Brandstetter."

"Good." He wanted that. He flapped into the bathrobe. Under his feet the floor felt clammy. He opened the door. Beyond the heavy white arches the rain-drenched leafage of the patio garden sparkled in sunlight. He squinted. Between him and the dazzle, a young Japanese smiled and held out a black tray painted with Mexican flowers and birds. On the tray steamed a painted pottery jug. There was a cup to match, a spoon, packets of sugar and powdered cream. Dave didn't take the tray. He said, "Your name's Ito, isn't it?"

"Yes, sir."

57

Joseph Hansen

Dave jerked his head. "Come in. I want to talk to you." The boy came in and put the tray down on a coffee table that had patterned tiles set into its top. Dave shut the door. "You worked for Fox Olson once, right?"

Dave's portable typewriter stood in its case on the floor by the coffee table. The boy looked at it, then at him. "Are you a reporter?" he asked. "I can't tell you much. I only worked for him one day."

"I'm an insurance investigator." Dave picked up the crumpled cigarette pack from the bedside stand. He held it out. The boy shook his head. Dave set a cigarette in his own mouth. "Last Christmas, was it?"

"That's right." The boy took a matchbook from his white jacket and lit the cigarette. Quick and graceful. "Mrs. Olson hired me. As a surprise for him."

"Thanks." Dave bent and poured coffee from the jug. It smelled great. "Was he surprised?"

"Very." The boy grinned. He had beautiful teeth. "He almost fell down."

"But he wasn't pleased? Look, if you get another cup . . ."

"It's okay," Ito said. "I've already had enough coffee to surf in." He had no Japanese accent. Strictly California. He blinked thoughtfully. "He seemed pleased. Mrs. Olson told me he was. That was Christmas Day." He raised his shoulders, held his hands out palms up. "Next morning—bop! You're fired."

"No reasons given?" Dave sat down on the edge of the bed, blew at the coffee, sipped it.

58

"No reasons." Ito smiled. "Just a very fat check. Not two weeks' wages. Two months'. Mrs. Olson said she was very sorry, she'd made a mistake. She'd thought Mr. Olson would want me working for him. He didn't."

"Whose check? His?" The ashtray was full of butts. When he tapped ashes into it, Ito took it and emptied it into the frayed Indian basket by the dresser.

"Hers," he said, putting the ashtray back. "She handled the money. I heard somebody talking about that, Christmas Day."

"What else happened that day?"

The boy shrugged. "They had a lot of people in. It was a beautiful day. Clear and sunny like this. Only dry and warm. I was really happy. I mean, it's a nice house, beautiful surroundings. The kitchen was perfect. That's what bugged me worst. I never got a chance to cook a real meal there."

"You like to cook?" Dave asked. "You don't cook here."

"No. But it's a good job. I'm saving my chips. When I get enough I'll open my own restaurant."

"The Olsons paid you well?"

"Better than any job I ever had. And I liked them. Especially him. He was somebody else, man. Always, like, 'If it's convenient' and 'Don't go to any extra trouble' and 'When you have time' and 'Aren't you getting tired? Would you like a break? I can look after things. . . .' Always jumping up to help me whenever I came in sight with a tray. They were mostly out in the garden and around the pool. Even

59

if he was singing or something, he'd take time to ask me if I was okay, did I need anything. Great guy."

"Except he fired you," Dave said.

Ito laughed. "Yeah. And they talk about inscrutable Orientals."

"No incidents with him? Arguments? Criticism?"

"No." The boy frowned. "Unless . . . I don't know whether you'd call it an incident, exactly. But after I got everything cleared up that night, real late, I was getting ready to sack out. I'd just had a shower. He knocked at my door and called my name and I said, 'Come in.' It was probably two-thirty, three by now. It'd been a long day. And he was kind of stoned. He opened the door and for a minute he just stood there staring at me. I was drying myself off. Then he said, 'Excuse me,' and started to back out.

"I asked if there was anything more I could do for him. He looked kind of funny for a minute. He didn't answer. Just stared with his mouth half open. Then finally he gave a smile like maybe he was feeling sick or something. He said, 'No, thanks, Ito. It was a very nice Christmas. . . .' And he turned and bumped into the door and mumbled, 'Thanks for all you did . . .' or something like that, and he was gone." The boy knelt, picked up the scattered scripts. "That was the last time we ever talked."

"It's a small town," Dave said. "You must have run into each other now and then."

"No. I don't move in the country club set. My speed is the movies and the bowling alley." Ito tamped the edges of the scripts on the dresser top and laid them in a neat stack. "If I was going to see him, it would almost have to be here. It was. Only a couple weeks ago. He drove in in that white T-bird of his. To see a guest. Guy from France. I was raking the garden. Mr. Olson passed me. He nodded and smiled. That was all." Ito frowned and sighed. "Just the same, I'm sorry he's dead. He was the nicest guy I ever expect to meet. . . ."

In the sunlit Daffodil Café, while Dave ate scrambled eggs and fresh country sausage, the little yellow plastic radio played Fox Olson again. Telling one of his stories this time. A lot was missing when you read them to yourself. The book would be funny. But a better idea would have been to put the stories on disks. Olson's easy, dry delivery gave them a—what word did he want?—drollness that print never could.

On the stools along the counter, at the tables in the booths, truck drivers, shopkeepers, ranch and vineyard hands grinned and chuckled and guffawed, forgetting the good coffee, the bacon and buckwheat cakes, the buttery breakfast rolls growing cold in front of them.

The story was about Aunt Minnie Husk, who, when the Cottonwood Corners water tower was toppled by beavers who'd mistaken the props for saplings, used the tank as a mold in which to bake the world's biggest cupcake, and how the resulting invasion of the town by millions of mice had been solved by the providential arrival of owls, "who gorged themselves till they were too heavy to fly. They could only sit on the ground and belch. . . ."

Dave had read it and laughed at it last night. He laughed now, all over again. Next to him sat a pair of high-school girls, Cokes in front of them, books in their laps. One was pretty and dark and wore braces on her teeth. The other was red-haired, freckled and fat. Pinned to each of their blouses was a big orange-and-blue campaign button: OLSON FOR MAYOR. When the story ended and a cigarette commercial twanged and everybody began eating again, Dave nodded at the buttons.

"Isn't it a little late for that?"

The pretty one gave him a cold look. "No. Everyone in school's wearing them. We loved him."

"Anyway," the freckled one said, "we don't think he's dead."

Dave nearly choked on his coffee. "You don't? Why not?"

The pretty one said dramatically, "Because his body was never found. Only his car."

"So I heard." Dave lit a cigarette. The tiny counter ashtray was yellow plastic. It looked flammable. He shook the match out carefully. "But if he's not dead, what happened to him?"

The freckled girl was poking a pair of bent paper straws among the melting ice chips in the bottom of her glass, noisily sucking up the last drops of sweetness. She stopped that for a second to say, "He was kidnapped."

"You're kidding. By whom? What for?"

"Mayor Chalmers, of course." The pretty girl was disgusted to have to explain anything so obvious. "Till the election's over."

62

"Come on, Lou Ann." The fat girl got off her stool. "If I'm late again, my mom will confiscate my tapes."

Picking up her books, Lou Ann told Dave, "Doreen's got every Fox Olson broadcast—"

"Till school started." Doreen made the correction over her shoulder, hurrying toward the Daffodil's screen door. There was a lot of her. All of it jiggled.

The street was as dry now as if it had never rained. By afternoon it would be dusty. Cars parked on the bias in Pima. He nosed his to the high curb between a pair of identical, mud-crusted pickup trucks piled with empty orange crates. The building he faced was old red brick. Two stories. On the downstairs windows peeling gilt lettering read PIMA VALLEY SUN. When he was on the sidewalk he saw through the windows that the paint inside was time-darkened, the desks and woodwork nicked. The morning was already warm and the front door stood open and sounds came out, jangle of telephones, stammer of two-finger typing, chitter of linotypes. He passed. He wanted the other door, the one with the KPIM logo on it.

He went in and climbed straight stairs into air-conditioned silence. The place smelled of newness and success. It glowed with clean light from fluorescent tubes masked by frosted glass. Underfoot the blue-green speckled carpeting was deep. The white walls and ceiling were cushiony with thick, fibrous plaster. Long rectangles of double plate glass looked into studios and control rooms where equipment glinted, records turned, shirt-sleeved men laughed without sound. Down the hall, somebody used a door. Thick and heavy, it sighed, closing.

In Hale McNeil's office floor-to-ceiling drapes, crisp blue-and-green-striped, shut out the view of ugly Main Street. The furniture was burnished steel and saddle leather. On the white wall hung a big Peter Hurd painting. McNeil wore buckskin-colored corduroy on his big frame, pockets leather-edged, modified cowboy style, expensive. His face was tanned and rugged, his dark hair handsomely gray at the temples. Dark brows and lashes made his blue eyes startling. The eyes mocked Dave.

"Thorne tells me you don't think Fox is dead."

Dave gave a small amused shrug. "Neither does the student body of Pima High. None of them at your house?"

"Grown and gone," McNeil said. "But . . . I suppose at that age he'd have worn the fool button. Probably tacked the poster up in his room too."

"Which, of course, his mother would have loved."

McNeil's face hardened. "His mother and I were divorced when Tad was fifteen months old. The reason? She was a drunk and a tramp. Prettiest girl in the graduating class of Pima High School, June 1939." His mouth twisted. "A drunk and a tramp."

"Who raised the boy? You, by yourself?"

"My folks. They did their best. So did I. But . . . there's an old saying: Wash a dog, comb a dog, still a dog. I don't know what's become of him. Don't care."

"But you do know about Mayor Chalmers's kidnap plot?"

"All. And now you come along with something even wilder. Fox cracked up his car to make it look as if he'd been killed, and walked away from everything. Why?"

"I keep asking," Dave said. "Somebody will tell me."

"I hope so. Nothing would please me more than to have him back here." McNeil glanced at his watch, pushed a button on his desk. Music came into the room. Fox Olson's guitar, Fox Olson's voice. Another harmless, tuneful, mildly clever little Western. Probably Olson's own. McNeil let it play itself out, then, when an announcer began talking, switched off the speaker. "I can use all of that I can get. You'd know what I mean if you'd seen this place a year ago. Dingy, like downstairs. I mean, we were broadcasting, we were making a profit, but——"

"Why did you cancel it after the car crash?"

McNeil's eyes were steady on him. "You know the answer to that. It was a matter of taste."

"But the listeners didn't figure it that way."

"As far as they were concerned it was all a dark plot." McNeil laughed soundlessly and shook his head. "Funny as hell, you know. I mean, the old ladies hollering about a Fox Olson blackout on KPIM, the kids with their cheap TV-inspired kidnap plot, and now you. I mean, if you'd known Fox . . . He was open and candid as a child. He had no more dark side to him than——than the sun."

"What about Mayor Chalmers?" Dave wondered. "Does he have a dark side?"

"Lloyd?" McNeil threw back his head and

65

laughed. It took him a minute to straighten his face. "No, Mr. Brandstetter. I'm afraid not. Lloyd's all shoulders. All"—he thrust out his jaw and made his voice gruff—"'Let's get the God damn job done!' The type that built the West. Lloyd could no more connive than he could hook doilies. Anyway, he never took Fox's running against him seriously. I doubt if he even noticed."

"Did you take it seriously?"

Amused, McNeil gave a quick headshake. "No. It was a gag to start with. Fox was rambling on one morning on the air about a mayoralty race in Cottonwood Corners—his imaginary small town, you know?"

Dave nodded. "Mrs. Olson lent me some scripts."

"Great, aren't they?" McNeil asked it mechanically. "Well, it gave me an idea. Just a promotional idea was all. Why not start a campaign over the station, Fox Olson for mayor?"

"And it got out of hand?"

"Did you ever have a kite pull you right off the ground when you were a kid? Then you know the feeling. But . . ." He shrugged. "We decided to go along with the gag. Fox went through the signing-up routines. And for the first time in the memory of a lot of the younger citizens of Pima, Lloyd Chalmers had somebody running against him for his office. His. Believe me. He built half this town. Nobody's going to disabuse him of the idea that he owns it. Not soon."

"But . . . he didn't take the campaign seriously?"

"Ask him," McNeil said. "He'll laugh at you."

"Was anybody going to vote for him? Olson, I mean."

McNeil chuckled. "Just everybody old enough."

"And then what? Did he want to be mayor of Pima?"

"I think he did." McNeil narrowed his eyes, tugged his lower lip. "Yes, I think he got to taking it kind of seriously after a while. But . . ." He shook his head, gave a crooked smile and stood up. "How could he?" McNeil walked to a filing cabinet, pulled open a drawer, brought out a fat manila folder. He laid it on the desk in front of Dave. "Look at these."

Expensive stationery. Lavish multicolored imprints. Dave turned over letter after letter. Radio. Would Fox Olson come and guest for a week with Arthur Godfrey on his morning show, tell some of his hilarious stories, sing a few songs? Television. Would Fox Olson do a segment for Ed Sullivan? Would Fox Olson consider dramatizing the Cottonwood Corners stories for a series, would he star in them himself? Records. Would Fox Olson record a dozen of his songs? Las Vegas. Would Fox Olson appear twice nightly in the Rodeo Room? Concert management firms. Motion picture studios . . . Dave closed the folder and looked up.

McNeil asked, "Where would he get time to be mayor?"

"Was he going to do all these things?" Dave tapped the folder.

"Are you kidding? My Christ, man, Fox Olson had been slaving a lifetime for success. Before he got this program I'd swear he was a man ready to put a bullet through his head. He'd given up. If it wasn't for his wife—" McNeil broke off. "Sorry. The answer is yes, he was going to do all these things. The record contract was already signed. With Dot. The rest of it was waiting till we could figure out a way to find time. See, Fox refused to do anything that would interfere with what he considered his obligation to me. KPIM came first. Hell, he hadn't even taken a vacation in a year and a half."

"I see," Dave said. Then, "What about the man from France? What kind of an offer was that?"

"How?" McNeil looked blank.

"Olson spoke to a man from France a couple of weeks ago. Somebody who'd come here to see him. Stayed at the Pima Motor Inn. Olson talked to him there. He didn't say anything to you about it?"

"Not that I remember." McNeil's phone rang and he reached for it. "Excuse me."

"I'll go," Dave said. And went.

8

The sun was hot. On a flat, smooth stretch of lawn a gaunt old man threw his cane. Hard and a long way. Two dogs chased it, big lean dogs, hounds of some kind. Rough blue-gray coats. They moved clumsily, like rusty machines. But fast. One of them got the cane and came back with it to the old man. It was a heavy cane but in the dog's jaws it looked fragile. The other dog stood where the cane had been and made a hoarse, rumbling sound that was supposed to be barking. The old man took the cane from the first dog and grabbed its collar. He heaved the cane to the other dog. Holding the collar hampered his throw so the cane didn't go as far this time. The free dog shambled to it, picked it up, came back with it.

Dave had been following the housekeeper, a middle-aged Mexican woman, square-built, the color and hardness of mahogany. There was flour on her hands, her apron, a streak of it in her hair, and when they came through the kitchen there was the smell of baking. Now as they neared the old man Dave could hear him breathing hard. The Mexican woman said, "The cane is to help you walk. You will kill yourself, throwing—"

69

"Oh, go back in the house." The old man spoke without even glancing at her. "Leave me be." He bent and took the cane from the second dog. "God damned rain kept me penned up inside for ten days. Man's got to have exercise. Dogs got to have exercise." He threw the cane again. It cut the air with a whining sound. The dogs creaked after it. The old man turned, grinning like a kid, a sick kid. "Hell, Carmelita, I never felt better in my—" He saw Dave. His face kept the smile the way an old barn keeps a sign. "Howdy?" It was a question.

Dave told him who he was and what he wanted. Loomis's eyes went prairie flat. "Clear off," he said. "Git. Go home and tell your outfit my son-in-law is dead."

"If he's dead," Dave said, "where's his body?"

Loomis's leather mouth opened but it said nothing. He shut it with a click of false teeth and sourly held out his hand. It was bone and gristle, very big, a plow hand. One of the dogs brought back the cane. It had a brown rubber tip. The old man took it, leaned on it and headed for the house, which was ugly Spanish colonial, fierce white in the sun. The cold bare room he called his office had only one decoration on the wall. A shotgun in a rack. He sat at a blank-looking green metal desk in a metal posture chair that squeaked. He nodded at a metal straight chair. Dave sat on that.

"All right," Loomis said, "his body should have been in that there wash. It wasn't. But he never run off. That just plain don't make sense."

"What does make sense?"

Loomis's slat shoulders moved inside the buttoned-up sweater that said, as much as anything about him, that he was a sick old man. "Maybe Lloyd Chalmers killed him."

Dave narrowed his eyes. "Are you serious?"

"There's a new junior college going to be built in Pima. That'll mean a multimillion-dollar construction contract. Lloyd'll be due for that, like he's due for every building job that comes along around here."

"Aren't there sealed bids?"

"Lloyd's always turn out to be the lowest." Loomis's smile was wry and didn't last. "There's a freeway coming through this valley too, one way or another. They're after me for a strip of my land. . . ." He swiveled the stiff little chair and stared out the window at the staked vine rows slanting up toward the brushy humps of mountain. "But that don't make no never mind. Wherever they route it, Lloyd'll get the contract. Provided he's in charge of things at city hall."

"Who would get the contracts if he wasn't? If Fox Olson had won the election?"

"No *if* about it." The old man faced him, proud. "He had it won. Lloyd knew that. He's pretty took up with what a great man he is, but he ain't stupid."

"He'd resort to murder?"

Loomis's laugh was a crackle of dry twigs, but it didn't change his face. His forehead furrowed. "Only thing wrong is, if he did, he'd do a good job. No loose ends. He'd never fake a car crash, then take away the driver's body. Naw . . ." The big dogs sprawled gaunt at Loomis's feet, flat on their sides, like starvation victims. The old man leaned down and stroked one of them. Regret was in his voice. "I'd like for the son of a bitch to get the gas chamber. But he won't. Leastways not for this."

Dave asked, "Why the deep affection for Lloyd Chalmers?"

"I'm a dirty, ignorant Okie to him. Was to start with, always will be. The Chalmers clan had been the big power in Pima for seventy years before I come along. Me, Hap Loomis—I'm kind of a bad dream, far as them and the McNeils and their crowd are concerned. They think one of these mornings they'll wake up and find me gone. Used to be a lot of Japs out here before the war. Never looked down on them like they do on me. Hell, I own half this valley. I could buy and sell the lot of them. But let me show up out at their God damn country club and they scatter like pullets when a skunk gets in the henhouse. . . ." It was a big jug of bitterness but now he tired of pulling at it and set it down. "What was it you asked me?"

"Why wouldn't Chalmers get the contracts even if Fox Olson became mayor? Fox wasn't in the building business."

"His son-in-law is. Starting."

"Phil Mundy? Is he capable? He's awfully young."

"Twenty-three. But he's already Chalmers's chief accountant. Started building an apartment before he even married."

"Ambitious," Dave said. "Do you like him?"

Loomis's smile was one-cornered. "I never feel

real easy about a man that's too smart with figures. My granddaughter Gretchen come to me for a loan. I told her no. Not for Phil Mundy."

"You didn't like her marrying him?"

"You seen that mother of his, that crippled kid?" Loomis snorted. "Feeling sorry for a man's a piss-poor reason to marry him."

"Did she get the loan from her father?"

"He couldn't give it to her. Thorne managed the money."

"Wouldn't she lend it?"

"She wouldn't even speak to Gretchen. She liked her marrying Phil Mundy the way I liked her marrying Fox Olson. That's something, ain't it? Life plays funny tricks."

"Sometimes not so funny," Dave said.

Loomis's muddy eyes regarded him wisely. "Them are the ones you got to laugh at hardest."

I never will, Dave thought, *not about Rod dying.* He said, "There was somebody you wanted Thorne to marry. She told me. But she didn't tell me who."

"Hale McNeil. It started when they was in high school. He took her out three, four times. Thorne had to sneak to do it. She was too young, only fifteen. When I found out about it, I told Charlie McNeil unless he stopped Hale I'd horsewhip the boy. McNeil didn't like it coming from me, but I had right on my side. Hale laid off—"

"And married someone else," Dave nodded.

"Mildred Fisher. Cheap tinsel. Things went all right till the army camp come. She couldn't keep away. Not from the honky-tonks either. Dozen of them on Main Street then. So . . . Hale shucked her." Mouth a wide, sad line, Loomis shook his head. "No surprise the boy turned out like he done."

"McNeil seems bitter about him," Dave said. "Why?"

"Ten, eleven years ago, local doctor got caught with the boy. Sex. Course Hale wanted to believe it was the man's fault. Wasn't. Come out at the trial. One high-school kid says Tad serviced the football team regular on the bus coming home nights from out-of-town games. There was half a dozen other stories. Shame of it killed Charlie. Hale—well, you don't mention Tad to Hale. Pima folks know that. You hear a joke about queers, don't tell him. He won't laugh."

"What became of Mildred Fisher—McNeil?"

"Story goes she was pregnant. Softhearted fellow by the name of Vince Mundy married her. He had a little place on the edge of town. Walnuts, some citrus. Real pretty. He'd been all right in time, had a good head on him. But Mildred finished that off. Finally he took to drinking as much as she did. And when that second baby—his own—was born a cripple, he walked out and never come back."

Dave blinked. "Then she's . . . Phil Mundy's mother?"

"Not much of a beauty now, is she?" Loomis snorted.

"No . . . But wait. There's something I don't understand. It was after the divorce that Hale McNeil came back for your daughter?"

Loomis nodded. "Soon as Thorne graduated from

74

high school, he asked her to marry him. She turned him down. I know she liked him. Loved his baby too. It was Pima she hated. When I tried to talk sense to her she flared up about rich men's sons being no account and a whole lot of horse shit like that. Anyhow"—he shifted his bones and the chair squeaked—"she done what she always done when I give her advice—the opposite. She run off to L.A. and married Fox Olson."

"What made McNeil offer Olson the radio job?"

"He done it for Thorne." Loomis cracked his big knuckles, methodically, thoughtfully, watching them. Then he looked up. "He's still in love with her."

"But why did she accept?"

Loomis shrugged. "Guess she was fed up with living on hope. When she got a look at how Hale McNeil lived . . ." He stared out the window again. There were runnels of shadow in the mountains now. "Hell, her man had nothing. Past forty years old and nothing to show. The top of the hill has got to be just ahead at forty. But Fox was still at the bottom. He wasn't going to reach the top pushing a typewriter. Guess she decided he might, pushing a guitar."

"How did he react to the offer?"

"Says thanks but no thanks"—Loomis grinned—"and hung up."

"You don't mean it."

"Fact." Loomis's eyes laughed, remembering. "Well, Thorne was all over him. It's the chance of a lifetime, she says, and he better grab it. He stands there with his jaw hanging. He can't figure it. A while back, when all these coffeehouses started up and all the kids singing and playing what they call folk songs, he wants to give up writing and go out do that. She near killed him. She claims she never, but I kind of guess he told it like it happened."

"So they argued about this?"

"Only till he was sure she meant it. Then he give a shrug and that grin of his and picked up the phone and says to Hale that he'll give it a try. And I'll hand it to him. He done fine. I did hand it to him. We got to be real good friends. And him being my son-in-law, a lot of people that wouldn't give me the time of day before, they turned real neighborly and respectful all of a sudden. Guess I could have run for mayor myself." He chuckled sourly, then tilted his head, blinking. "Queer thing, though. About Thorne. She never listened. I did." He jerked a work-flattened thumb at a radio on the desk, half buried among U.S. Agriculture Department bulletins. "Never missed him on the air. But Thorne—she couldn't have cared less."

9

She had on a clean cotton housedress today. Starchy. The faded pink cardigan over it had been washed so often it had no more shape left than she had. Her hair was combed and her face scrubbed. No makeup. Instead of a wine bottle there was a Bible in her hand. The big eyes that had been bleary with booze last night were clear now. More than clear. Bright. Too bright. Her smile clicked on. So did her voice, also too bright.

"It's Mr. Brandstetter, isn't it?"

She pushed open the screen. He stepped in. She didn't wear perfume. The smell was of some kind of medicinal soap.

"We met last night," he said.

"Yes." He knew now what the trouble was: the eyes didn't blink. The voice went on, a recorded message. "I'm an alcoholic. It's a sickness. But I'm winning. Prayer helps me. God helps me." She glanced down at the Bible and then laid it on the telephone stand.

"And your children?" he said.

"They're wonderful." Her smile was a rictus that belonged with a scream. "Aren't they wonderful? My beautiful boys. I don't know what I'd do without them."

"And your daughter-in-law? Is she beautiful too?"

"I'm so proud of her," Mildred Mundy said. "I couldn't have wished for a finer girl for my Phil."

"And so rich too," Dave said.

The eyes still didn't blink. The mouth made a big O. The tongue clucked. "Why, Gretchen's not rich. Her grandfather, sure. But she works for a living, typist at the United Growers. Money's not the important thing in this life. Love is." For a second the eyes and voice came humanly, bitterly alive. "I know. I was married to a rich man once." She didn't go on.

"Money seemed important to you last night. You followed me into a hard rain after that fifty thousand dollars Fox Olson left Gretchen."

"I wasn't myself last night." The eyes stared blank at him again. A puffy hand groped for the Bible and touched it like base. Then she started along the hall. "Buddy's waiting for you. You're nice to come play chess with him. Now that Phil's got his own building business along with his job and Fox is dead, Buddy gets lonesome."

"I get lonesome too." Dave followed her, the warped floor tilting under his feet. "And I don't get to play chess often." He said it loud and clear because the door to Buddy's room was shut.

Mildred Mundy opened it. Her voice had the terrible fake cheerfulness of a death ward nurse, a bad echo in Dave's mind. "Mr. Brandstetter's here, Buddy. Isn't that nice?"

"That's . . . nice." Buddy's smile was better than the human average. He sat in his steel tubular wheelchair, the chessboard in front of him, the wooden men in ranks. He wore a red sweatshirt and white corduroy pants and tennis shoes. Wore is the wrong word. They hung on him as if on a small, broken drying rack. Last night, wet from his bath, his hair had looked dark. It was fair, a shock of wheat. The eyes were still the color of rain. "Hi . . . Mr. . . . Brand . . . stetter." The name made for a lot of agonizing jaw work.

"Make it Dave." Dave smiled and sat down on the kitchen chair facing the boy. The chair was newly painted but the rungs were wired and it wobbled.

"Just call me if you want anything." Mildred Mundy went out and shut the door.

"Th . . . anks . . . Mama."

"I hope four was a good time." Dave glanced at the television set. "There isn't something you want to watch? I just picked my own time. That wasn't very considerate."

The boy's fine head did its slow, neck-straining roll while the unexpectedly deep voice spasmed and his mouth labored at shaping the speech. Chess was preferable to TV. Though he was grateful to Fox Olson for giving him the set, he didn't watch it much. It was moronic for the most part. He enjoyed reading. And KPIM played good music in the evenings.

"Good music? What about Mr. Olson's music? You don't like that?"

Buddy meant Bach and Bartok. Sure, he liked

Fox's music. Fox used to bring his guitar here and sing. It was better that way than on the radio, like cheerful conversation. But Fox hadn't taken it seriously himself. He liked Mozart and Mahler.

"Did he come here often?" But the boy was eyeing the chessmen. Dave reached for a pawn of each color so they could draw for white. But the white men were ranked on his side and Buddy said:

"Be . . . my guest."

Dave pushed his king's pawn and the boy countered the move. It took time because the small clean hand kept twisting out of control. But Dave waited, judging that if Buddy wanted help he would ask for it. Chess was no game to hurry anyway. Yes, Fox Olson had spent a lot of time in this room, had taken Buddy to films, driven him to his physical therapy sessions at the hospital, replaced his clumsy old wooden wheelchair with this flash one, a standard-model typewriter with the electric that was better for writing because you could think about words instead of motions. What did he write? Haiku . . . He took Dave's knight with a bishop from a far corner.

Dave groaned. "I told you I was a potzer."

"You aren't. You're think. . . ing." In the straining, tormented young face, the eyes were steady. "About Fox." Gretchen had told Buddy why Dave was in Pima, that he didn't believe Fox was dead but had only run away.

"What about you?" Dave asked. "What do you think?"

"May . . . be. If I . . . could I . . . would." Buddy

glanced at the ceiling, the rows of bright license plates.

"That how you travel?" Dave asked.

Buddy gave his loud bray of laughter but the eyes were sad. It was how he traveled. He lay in bed and thought about the places the license plates came from. He knew a lot about them from reading the *National Geographic*s. He had plates from every state, including Alaska and Hawaii. Phil had got them for him over the years. The boy named Sandy, at the Signal station—whose girl friend worked for Fox—had contributed a couple. Including Mexico. Buddy's first foreign one. The second Fox had brought. Dave saw it in the ceiling corner, a long black rectangle with white numerals. France. He looked at the boy.

"Where did he get it?"

About two weeks ago, Fox had come here with a stranger. They had driven into the Mundys' yard under the walnut trees in the man's car. A Ferrari. With French license plates. Fox had introduced the man to Buddy as an old friend, simply as Doug, no last name. Anyway, the man wasn't French. He was American. Only he had lived in France for a long time. Something to do with NATO. He was nice. He'd taken Buddy for a ride. They'd driven out the highway. It was the first sports car the boy had ever ridden in. His eyes shone, remembering. On the straightaway Doug had opened it up. The speedometer needle had passed 120 before traffic had slowed them down. When they got back here, Doug, at Fox's suggestion, had given Buddy the license plate . . . He pushed a rook. Dave's king was in check.

"Maybe . . ." Buddy said, "Fox went . . . to Fr . . . ance."

Dave blinked. "Why would he go to France?"

"He was . . . hap . . . py . . . with Doug." Buddy watched his hand moving like a slow, stunned, naked little animal, setting the white pieces back in place. "I told . . . Phil . . . I nev . . . er saw Fox . . . laugh the way . . . he did . . . that day."

A smoldering Valentino in white riding breeches ought to have been waiting in the motel office. It was a silent-movie set. Slot windows in deep white walls, guarded by grilles of black iron. Black carved beams, black iron chandelier. Floor of square red tiles. Tapestry-backed chairs with brass studs and gold fringe. But it wasn't Valentino. It was Ito in a tidy white jacket.

He took a registration card out of a green file box and laid it on the counter top, which was inlaid with painted tiles. The name was lettered on the card with a black felt-tip pen. Dashing. *Douglas Sawyer. Los Angeles.*

Ito said, "It was a Ferrari. Red." Red, dying sunlight slanted into his eyes and he narrowed them, watching Dave copy the address and license number. "A car like that must cost a bundle."

"Around fifteen thousand dollars," Dave said.

Ito whistled softly. "Who was this cat? Somebody important?"

"Possibly. At least to me." Dave laid a dime on the counter. "May I make a local call?"

"Sure." Ito slid the phone toward him.

While Dave checked a number in his address book, he asked Ito, "Do you know whether anybody else saw him while he was here?"

"You mean came to see him?"

Dave dialed. "I mean just what I said."

"Well . . ." Ito shrugged. "Sandy Webb, the kid at the Signal station. He saw him. I heard him raving about the car at the bowling alley one night. Sawyer bought gas from him."

Dave smiled thanks and Thorne Olson answered the phone. "I'm just checking on my memory," he told her. "Didn't you tell me your husband once had a friend named Sawyer, Doug Sawyer?"

"Is this Mr. Brandstetter?"

"Sorry to bother you," he said.

"Yes." Her voice was chilly, impatient. "The answer to your question is yes. They were very close friends. They attended art school together. The Provence School."

"And didn't you say Sawyer was a flier in the war?"

She sighed. "And was killed on a bombing mission over Europe, yes. But I don't see what this can possibly—"

He cut across her annoyance. "Doug Sawyer is alive, Mrs. Olson. He was here in Pima only two weeks ago. Your husband talked to him at the Pima Motor Inn."

"I don't believe it."

"The registration card is here with his name on it. Your husband was seen going into his unit."

"But . . ." Her voice climbed a step. "He would have told me. Fox worshiped Doug Sawyer. Why, if he had . . ."

"Yes?"

Her tone hardened. "Is this supposed to have some connection with Fox's death?"

"Disappearance," Dave said. "I don't know. When I do, I'll bother you again." He hung up and looked at Ito. "I'm checking out." He turned for the door.

"You think you'll find Mr. Olson?"

"Maybe." The brown boy was reflected in the thick beveled glass of the door. Dave told the reflection, "One living dead man ought to be able to lead me to another."

And he went out and shut the door.

10

Three hours later, at San Fernando, he caught up with the rain again. It hissed under the tires as he curved along the freeway into Hollywood. He hadn't eaten and he needed to. He had lost too much weight. Traffic on Sunset was heavy and slow. When he reached Romano's it was late. There were only a couple of cars left in the parking lot. Reflecting neon signs, the puddles he stepped through were like paintings drowning in ink. The familiar stained-glass windows smiled welcome. He pushed into steamy warmth, good smells of cheese and garlic. Fat Max was there to take his coat. Big smile full of gold fillings.

"Mr. Brandstetter. You're a stranger. Where you been? Where's Mr. Fleming?"

"Dead, Max. Cancer." And when the old Italian's good-natured face crumpled with shock and pity, Dave turned fast for the bar. "Make it lasagne with sausages tonight. Garlic toast. Big salad. Vino. Give me twenty minutes."

"I'm-a so sorry about Mr. Fleming. We'll miss him."

"Thanks." The bar, dark woods and leathers, stained-glass lanterns, was not big but it was nearly empty. Rain could do that to business in L.A. There was only one other customer. A woman. He noticed her without looking at her. The bartender he didn't know. That was good. He wouldn't have to say it again, about Rod. It wasn't martini weather but that was what he ordered, hoping it would make him hungry. He started a cigarette and went to work on the drink.

Then the woman slid onto the stool next to his. This could happen at Romano's? Still, he'd never sat here alone before. Rod had always been with him. He picked up the martini and had one foot on the floor when he smelled her perfume and knew who she was. The scent was Russia Leather, had been for twenty years. The woman was Madge Dunstan, had been for forty-five years. Old friend. She had introduced him and Rod to Romano's in 1948. He turned back. "Madge," he said.

Her smile was gently reproachful. "I've been worried about you. I phoned every day as I said I would." At the funeral she'd told him she didn't expect him to answer. She'd rung the bell to let him know she was there and caring. "Then I thought I'd better look at you in the flesh and I drove to your house and your car was gone and I started worrying."

"I should have told you. That was rude as hell. I went back to work." A cigarette hung in the corner of her wide humorous mouth. He lit it for her. "A policyholder disappeared up in San Joaquin Valley. I'm only down here now to follow up a lead."

Freckled and bony, her hand squeezed his. "I'm glad you're all right."

"I'm not all right," he said. "I'm working at it but I'm a long way from it."

"You're terribly thin," she said.

"I'm counting on Max to cure that." He drank and looked at her. "What are you doing here so late? And alone. Where's the golden girl?" He didn't remember the girl's name. She was sun-toasted and had smooth boy features and muscular legs and strong white teeth and a loud laugh. But so did most of Madge's girls. He had watched maybe a score of them come and go.

She took away her hand and poked at the ashtray with her cigarette. Her mouth tried for a wry smile. "Gone. Not with the wind. With the rain. And I?" She had a husky laugh that often turned to a cough. It did so now. She shook her head ruefully. "I'm sitting here going through the motions of feeling sorry for myself and lonely and forsaken. Repeating a ritual I began too many years ago to count, and perfected through a number of farewell performances. But actors wear out roles. I've worn out this one. I can't do it anymore. The sketch wasn't hard when I understood it was fifty percent fake. When I was young enough to know at the back of my mind there'd be another girl soon and, if that one left, another . . . I don't know that anymore. So the fun's gone out of mourning." She glanced at him quickly. "Sorry. Wrong word."

"Don't apologize." He gave her a crooked smile. "If you're shrewd, you're shrewd. Come on. Sit with me while I eat." He got off his stool and handed her off hers. In tailored slacks and an expensive duffle coat, she looked young, her gauntness passed for slimness. The soft lights helped. She'd been putting booze away and walked a little unsteadily. It was all right. He respected her excuse. "I'm sorry you're hurting." He held a chair for her at a corner table that was lit by a fat amber candle. "But I'm glad I found you here."

"So am I." She picked up a smile and discarded it. "Funny thing . . . I have that feeling whenever I see you. Always have." She cocked her head, blinking. "Actually, I don't know anybody else I can say that about."

"The girl, whoever she is, when she's new."

Her mouth tightened at one corner. "The new wears off."

Max waddled over. "Will Miss Dunstan eat now?"

Dave stared. "You mean she hasn't?"

"Miss Dunstan," Madge said, "will steal some of Mr. Brandstetter's garlic toast. And that will be enough for Miss Dunstan, thanks, Max."

Max shook his head in worried disapproval but he never argued. He went away. Somewhere he had a record player hidden. Now he made it work. Songs from a Neapolitan street organ. Verdi, jangling and off key. To Dave it was like a blow in the stomach. He half stood. Startled, alarmed, Madge caught his sleeve. "What's wrong?"

"The stupid music. I wish he hadn't done that. Jesus! Italians!" But it wasn't Max's fault. Dave raked a hand through his hair and dropped into the chair again. "Funny." His laugh was bleak. "Many's the time I've sat here and sworn at Rod under the cover of that beautiful, awful record. Now he's not here, it breaks my heart." Tears blurred his eyes. He looked away quickly, across the muted room to where the steel doors of pizza ovens gleamed beyond a high brick counter. "But Verdi's going to be around for a long time, isn't he? Traviata's going to keep dying. I'm going to have to learn to ignore it." Madge's face was scribbled with sympathy. He smiled. "Did you know she was a terrible liar, said lying kept her teeth white?"

Madge squinted. "Who?"

"Marguerite Gautier. Camille. Traviata." The salad came. He busied his hands with the oil, the vinegar, the pepper mill. Watching him, she mused aloud:

"Maybe it does. I've always been wedded to the truth. You should see my dentist bill. Whereas Cuff"—that was the sunburned girl's improbable name—"Cuff could lie from dawn till dark and 'Look, Ma, no cavities!'" Her expression hardened abruptly. "You know, Davey, I'm sick of liars. I'm sick of kids. I'm sick of pretty girls who trade on their prettiness. I am F-E-D, fed, U-P, up."

He spoke with a mouth full of salad. "Pick an ugly one next time." He dabbed olive oil from his chin with his napkin. "Find some lonely, simple-hearted plain Jane of forty. I've told you that before."

"And I've told you a relationship without sex isn't worth having."

It was an old debate. It came up regularly. Every time Madge was reassembling the broken pieces after an affair. They were always that with Madge.

None of them lasted more than a few months. He always gave her the same advice. Find somebody your own age and mentality and background. She always ignored it. Next week, next month, another junior-grade design student, paint-smeared helper in the silk-screen shop, would-be actress, swimmer, model, tennis player, singer . . .

Madge was herself a successful and well-heeled designer of textiles and wallpapers. Hard-working, clever, an achiever, somebody with a lot to give. Easy, amusing, informed, none of the usual lesbian paranoia. Decent too, down to the ground. But the nice girls she found to bed could give no more than sweetness, which you can't live on. And the rest, the majority, were simply takers. It had been a sad pageant to watch.

He asked, "Why should it have to be without sex?"

"Because you can't make yourself want sex with somebody. It happens or it doesn't happen." She gave a sour, soundless laugh. "For me it always happens wrong. You just know Keats died young. Beauty is not truth and truth is not beauty. The two words don't even belong in the same dictionary."

The wine came, the garlic toast, the steaming lasagne. The waiter brought two glasses. Madge began work on hers right away. There was salad left in the big wooden bowl. She attacked that too, and tore into the garlic toast. They ate in silence for a few minutes. Then, when he'd filled her glass again, she picked it up and studied him over its rim. Very grave.

"I'm through chasing beauty. Cuff was the last."

Dave told her, "There was a guy in the army. Name of George Starkovich. One of the ugliest men I ever saw. Squat. Hairy. But inside he was beautiful. He was one of the nicest things that ever happened to me in my life."

She shut her eyes a second and nodded. "I remember. You've told me. Any number of times. The point is lost on me, Davey. Sorry. If it can't be beautiful I don't want it. And if it is beautiful, it's not worth having." She drank from the glass, set it down businesslike, and her tone was brisk. "Granted, it took me a long time to figure it out. Figure it out I have done. And things are going to be different from now on."

The lasagne was as good as ever. Maybe better. He had a mouthful of it and could only raise his eyebrows to ask her to go on.

"Sex and companionship are mutually exclusive. Too bad. But a fact. Anyway a fact for me. However . . . one gets more important as the other gets less. Right?"

He held out his hands and shrugged.

"I'm getting old, Davey. O-L-D, old."

He swallowed. "You, Madge? Never."

"Me most of all," she said. "When the thought of merry girlish chatter is enough to send you pawing through the medicine chest for that old set of ear plugs, you've had it. You're old. You begin wanting some nice, quiet, grown-up company. Somebody restful. Sex? You dimly remember something about it. A game for kids. Strenuous. You want to stretch limp in your easy chair and listen to Mozart quartets."

"You're getting at something," he said. "Sideways. That's not like you, Madge."

"I know it." She looked away. Her fingers turned the wineglass by its stem. It tipped and she righted it clumsily and fussed for longer than needful with the red splash on the cloth. Then she looked up at him and her eyes were little-girl wide. "I'm talking about living with you."

He could only stare.

"You're alone. Nobody's ever going to take Rod's place. You've got to leave that house. You know you do. And I'm alone too. And I've got lots of space." She had—big white rooms full of sunlight and the sea gleaming blue beyond. "We've been friends since man descended from the trees. We're comfortable together. . . ." She lowered her head but her eyes were still on him, anxious. "Aren't we?"

She meant this. In dead earnest. And he was sorry. Because she was wrong. About herself, for openers. Cuff had left scars but they would heal. About him, because somebody would take Rod's place. Who, he couldn't say. But he would find somebody. Until this minute he hadn't known that. He knew it now. He half rose, leaned across the table and kissed her forehead. Solemn and brotherly. Then he sat down again and took hold of her skinny hands.

"Do you know these lines, Madge? 'The weight of the world is love. Under the burden of solitude, under the burden of dissatisfaction, the weight, the weight we carry is love. . . .'"

She stared at him for a moment. Then tears brimmed her eyes and started down her face. She groped in her big over-the-shoulder handbag for Kleenex. She blotted the tears, blew her nose. Her mouth quivered. Her voice was thin and sad and wobbly.

"I wanted to set the weight down," she said.

He shook his head and gave her a small regretful smile. "Not bloody likely," he said.

I I

The snapshot was dog-eared and faded and had
lost its gloss. In bright sunlight a blond boy in ragged
swim trunks, and a smaller, dark boy in Levi's, shirt
open and flapping in the wind, grinned at the
camera, side by side. They stood easy, hipshot, arms
thrown over each other's shoulders, on a pier. A
gull swung above them. Beyond them, through
strong scaffolding, the ocean glinted. He had seen
scaffolding like that lately. Where?

"That was 1941. Twenty-six years ago. It doesn't
seem possible." The little pet-shop woman in her
flowered smock peered up at Dave. Her glasses were
thick, a circle of white cloth pasted inside one of
the lenses. The visible eye was black and bird-bright.
Birds surrounded her in shiny cages. Canaries, para-
keets, finches. Noisy flowers. "They spent the whole
summer at Bell Beach. One of them—I don't even
remember now if it was Fox or Doug—sold a dozen
silly, schoolboy cartoons to some pulp paper magazine, and so they had a few dollars." Her smile was
fond, remembering. "How excited they were."

"It had to be a long time ago." Dave studied the
photo. "Kids today don't grin like that."

"No, they don't, do they?" She nodded, troubled.

"It's as if they understand already that there isn't much in life to smile about." She sighed. "And that's a shame. They ought to be like birds."

Like a bird in trouble, a kettle shrieked in the back room. She led him there. The place was dim under forty-watt bulbs. It smelled of seed, alfalfa, sawdust—bird food, rabbit pellets, cage litter. Paper barrels, bulging sacks, unopened cartons, dusty unsold aquariums, cages in swaths of brown paper. Behind chicken wire, guinea pigs hopped over the backs of tortoises. A taffy-colored cocker spaniel nursed wriggling pups. A sick monkey hunched by a rain-gray window.

The hot plate stood on a shelf beside a scarred refrigerator. There was an open pound paper box of sugar on the shelf, a jar of powdered cream substitute. She fixed mugs of instant coffee and cracked open a cellophane box to get him a little red plastic spoon to stir his with. They went into the shop again. Hard, bright surfaces under glaring fluorescents. Bouquets of loud plastic flowers. A bubbling green fish tank. Dave lit a cigarette and picked up the photo.

"Doug looks smaller than Fox. Was he younger?"

"Only four months. Fox's birthday was July, Doug's was November. But Doug was never strong. He had rheumatic fever when he was seven. He was delicate. We had to be careful with him always."

"But he ended up in the Air Force," Dave said.

Her laugh was brief and mirthless. "It was a shock. The doctor had sworn his heart was damaged and it'd never be right again. Course, we didn't keep running back and back to the doctor. Couldn't afford it, in the first place. And after all, he never had spells or anything. Just colds and little stomach upsets—the usual. And I watched him to be sure he never overdid. He was naturally quiet, anyway. Never cared for sports."

"And his heart mended."

She snorted. "Doctors! There probably wasn't anything wrong with it in the first place." A myna bird by the front window threw back its head and laughed. It sounded human. She called, "That's right, Rudyard," blew at her coffee, frowned. "It upset Fox something awful. He wasn't taken, you know. Into the service, I mean. Can't say why. And neither of them expected Doug would qualify. Nobody did. Fox went over to the enlistment place with him. When they came home you've never seen such long faces."

She sipped gingerly at the coffee, set the mug down and blinked at Dave. "Do you know . . . I never knew two people as close as those two boys. Not in my whole life." She gave a little thoughtful headshake. "And when Doug came home from Europe and saw that story in the *Times*—it was just a paragraph, you know, about this radio entertainer going to run for mayor of some little ranch town—he yelled. Really. Right out loud. Jumped out of his chair and came running into the kitchen, flapping the paper, and threw his arms around me, and I swear I don't know whether he was laughing or crying."

There was a long ash on Dave's cigarette. She poked among the litter on the counter, cuttlebone, plastic-wrapped dog toys, catnip mice, and found an oval milk-glass birdbath and pushed it at him. "Of course," she went on, "I'd long ago lost track of Fox. He just dropped out of sight when Doug was reported killed. He'd stayed on at the art school, you know, but he left after that. When Doug turned up alive in a prison camp at the end of the war, I tried to find Fox, but he wasn't in the phone book. The aunt who raised him, church organist, she was dead, come to find out. So that was where my search ended. Didn't have time to look for him right then. Mr. Sawyer was in the hospital and I had my hands full with the shop. . . ."

Her face set, abused. "Then, when Doug didn't come home, decided to stay on in Europe and take the occupation job the government offered him"— her mouth pinched up and there was an edge of spite honed on self-pity to her voice—"I guess I decided Fox didn't matter anymore. Any more than I mattered. Alone here."

Dave stubbed out the cigarette. "Doug didn't ask about Fox in his letters to you?"

"Only in the first one, is all." She forgot her hurt. The single blackbird eye was keen on Dave's face. "And I thought of that when he showed all the excitement here, about Fox in the paper. Seemed queer after twenty-odd years. Why . . . he didn't even sit down to supper. I'd fixed him ham and scalloped potatoes, dish he used to just drool over. No, sir. He threw a handful of clothes into an airline bag and jumped in that *noisy* car, and chased off up the coast to find Fox."

"But he came back?"

"Oh, yes. He was only gone a day." The coffee was drinkable now. She swallowed some. "He said Fox has made quite a little success. Married . . ." Small, crooked smile. "Imagine. All these years. Got a grown daughter, married herself now. Fox . . ." She clucked disbelief. "He'll always be sixteen, seventeen, eighteen to me. Doug says he's losing his hair. He had so *much*. His aunt was always after him to get it cut. Asked me to back her up. I did, of course. But it seemed a shame. All that shaggy yellow hair. Pretty, I thought."

"Did Doug say he'd met Fox's wife?"

"Why . . ." She chewed her lip. "No, come to think of it, he didn't." She drank again, frowning. "That's odd, isn't it?" The fond smile returned. "Can't imagine what kind of girl Fox would marry. Seems—well, impossible." She laughed at herself. "But that's foolishness, of course. Why shouldn't he marry?"

"She's small, dark, slender." Dave tipped his head at the photo. "Like your son. He didn't marry?"

"Doug?" The smile, the little headshake regretted, apologized. "No. But he adopted a young French boy, war orphan. Jean-Paul Raideur. That's where Doug's interest in cars comes from. The boy was a mechanical—well, genius, I suppose you'd say. But Doug never cared about cars when he was that age. Oh, he and Fox had an awful old rattletrap they used to get to school in. But neither one of them could fix it when it broke down. And it broke down seems like every week or so. . . ." She laughed, recollecting. "But Jean-Paul . . . Doug housed and fed him and sent him through school. Then the army had an automotive training course and somehow Doug fixed things so he could be in that. Then, afterward, he bought him a car to race in. Cars. I think he broke every bone in his body one time or other. But he did win. I don't know how it works exactly, but if you win often you make all kinds of money. Then he was killed. Just about the time General de Gaulle shooed NATO out of France. All the same, I don't think Doug would have come home. Not if Jean-Paul hadn't died. At Le Mans it was."

The wound opened inside Dave's chest again. He turned and walked to the glass door and stared out at the empty street with the rain glazing it. A run-down neighborhood business district like a hundred others in sprawling Los Angeles. Shabby one-story stucco buildings. Hairdresser. Florist. Bicycle shop. Without turning, he said, "Now, then, you told me he's not here because he got a telephone call. Wednesday afternoon. October eighteenth."

"He'd been kind of quiet since he saw Fox. Depressed, I thought. But when that call came, well, I've never seen him so excited. His hands were shaking so that when he tried to hang up the receiver he dropped it. The whole phone fell on the floor. His eyes were shining, just shining. He went straight to his room and started packing.

"'Who was it?' I asked him. But he said he couldn't tell me. Nor what it was about, either. Well, I assumed it was the government calling him for a

99

job. He'd expected them to phone—only he didn't think he'd accept. But I guess it must have been a better offer than he'd expected.

"'Where will you be going?' I asked him. 'I hope not overseas again.' He came and gave me a little kiss on the cheek and a hug and said he was sorry but he couldn't tell me that either. So I just decided it was top secret. He promised he'd write me after he got settled."

Dave turned. "Has he written?"

"No, but it's only been a few days. . . ." She cocked her head, frowning, wary. "Mr. Brandstetter, you don't think that phone call was from Fox."

"Wednesday, October eighteenth, was the date Fox disappeared." Dave came back to the counter. "May I see your telephone directory?" She stooped and rummaged it from under the counter. Birdseed rattled out of it when he turned the pages looking for the area-code number of Pima. "I'd like to call long distance. The town where Fox lived. I thought I'd talked to everyone there who could tell me anything. Now I'm not so sure." He laid down the phone book, dug out his wallet and put a five-dollar bill into her hand. "This should cover the call." It would feed a lot of feathery dependents, but she hardly noticed it. Her stare was anxious. She gave a meager nod. When the Pima operator got him the number, the phone rang for a long time. He almost gave up. Then the voice was the one he wanted to hear, young, sullen.

"Signal station."

"This is Brandstetter, the dirty old man who gave your bird a hitch night before last. Remember?"

"She says you're a private eye. Figures. You can't get any dirtier than that."

"I'm an insurance investigator. Very clean-living. Fox Olson was insured for a hundred and fifty thousand dollars. I think he skipped out, split. You want to help me find him?" It sounded feeble in his own ears, as if he was trying to con a six-year-old. But a cynical kid is still a kid. He was vulnerable. Adventure. Excitement. Revenge. Just like on TV.

"Sure. Why not? The son of a bitch."

"Good. Do you remember a Ferrari gassing up at your place maybe two weeks ago?"

"Yeah. French plates."

"Did you see it only that once?" Dave swallowed dryness. "Or . . . did it come back?"

Pause. "It came back." Grudgingly. "You're sharp."

"The night Olson crashed his T-bird in the canyon?"

"Check. Late. Raining to beat hell. It didn't have the French plate in the front anymore."

"It's nailed up on Buddy Mundy's ceiling," Dave said. "Did you notice where the Ferrari went? Did it turn up the canyon?" His heart thudded.

"Yeah. I watched because it's such a bitchin' car. I stood there just to listen to the engine till I couldn't hear it anymore."

"And . . . you didn't hear it again?"

"I closed up right after that. Went home."

"How come you didn't tell the fuzz about this?"

"They never asked me."

Joseph Hansen

"Sure," Dave said. "Okay. Thanks."

"Shove the thanks. Send bread." Sandy hung up.

Dave put down the receiver. He told the little woman, "Doug was in Pima that night."

Light glinted off the thick lenses. "Are you saying my son would help Fox cheat your insurance company?"

Dave said gently, "If Fox asked him to, do you think he'd refuse?"

102

12

In his office on the tenth floor of the new glass-and-steel Medallion building on Wilshire Boulevard, Dave hung up the phone. Wearily. He'd been using it all afternoon. His hand was cramped. His ear felt bruised. He shook his head at the man standing in the doorway, lean, erect and ruddy. Only his white hair hinted at his age. Late sixties. He was Dave Brandstetter's father and the man Dave Brandstetter worked for. He dropped into a hairy white goat's-hide chair. His voice was as handsome as the rest of him.

"God knows," he said, "you've tried."

"The police haven't turned up any Ferrari in Fresno. That would be the nearest town to Pima with an airport you can call an airport. Just the same, I've had three of our people check all flights from there starting zero hours October nineteen. Also from the bay area. No luck."

"Obviously Sawyer owns a passport. Does Olson?"

"I couldn't reach his wife to confirm it. Nor McNeil, his what—boss, manager? Both away somewhere this afternoon. But I doubt he had one. He'd been poor until pretty lately. Bureau says no application is being processed for him. Which leaves Mexico or Canada."

"And explains why the car hasn't turned up abandoned somewhere. They're driving it."

"I hope so," Dave said. "Junking a Thunderbird's one thing. But a Ferrari? Painful idea."

"You tool down to the border," his father said. "It's possible one of the guards will remember a car like that. Especially with French tags."

"Thanks. I'll do that." But Dave was thinking that the United States of America is a big country: two hundred million people. If you wanted to lose yourself, you really wouldn't have to leave it. There was no point in saying so. They both knew it. He smiled and made the expected polite inquiry. About stepmother number nine, or was it ten? "How's Nanette?"

The older man snorted. "I'm preparing to shed Nanette. Someone, as the old fairy tale puts it, has been sleeping in my bed."

"That's too bad," Dave said.

"It could be worse." His father rose with a wry smile. "She could have caught me sleeping in somebody else's bed. That can be very costly."

"She lasted a long time," Dave said. "Three years? Four?" He took Old Crow from a cabinet that was metal patterned to look like wood. Chunky glasses. Ice cubes.

"Damn near five," his father said behind him. "She was beginning to bore me anyway."

"Drink?"

"Before driving? In weather like this? Haven't you learned anything from twenty years in the insurance game?"

"Twenty-two years." Dave drowned the cubes in the glasses, handed one to his father. "I've learned driving is so dangerous I haven't got the guts to do it sober." He grinned and lifted his glass.

"You can joke." His father's eyebrows signaled surprised approval. "That's good. I told you the smart thing was to get back to work. You're feeling better, aren't you?"

Dave said, "Somebody remarked last night that the fun goes out of mourning after a while."

His father sat down, making a face. "Not too tactful."

"The truth seldom is." Dave perched on a corner of his desk. "I'm all right."

His father tried the whiskey, started to speak, frowned, wasted time with a cigarette and a gold butane lighter. Finally, solemn, clearing his throat, he said, blunt, businesslike, "All right. Now he's gone. That infatuation's done with. You're forty-four years old. It's time you found a wife and settled down."

Dave laughed. "Look who's talking about settling down."

"Well, damn it, you know what I mean. Kids, a family. Future. I at least gave you life."

"A slipup and you know it," Dave said. "What is it you're getting at? You want to be a grandfather? That I find very difficult to believe."

"I don't see why."

"What the hell kind of genetic legacy are we supposed to bequeath to the world of tomorrow? An old satyr and a middle-aged auntie!"

His father winced. "You've got a very ugly mouth sometimes."

"I'm sorry," Dave said, "but you're not being honest and you know it. You don't mean a word of it. When you go all conventional and *Reader's Digest* like this, I don't know what to do—laugh or throw up."

"When you're older . . ." His father rose and he wasn't straight now. There was an old man's slump to his shoulders. Probably, Dave thought, intentional. ". . . you'll become aware that there is some kind of good purpose behind the conventions you sneer at."

"*I* sneer at!" Dave's laugh was impatient. "You've always considered them sacrosanct, of course. Especially the ones touching on Holy Matrimony."

"Maybe now I regret that. I'm not sure I could have done any differently if I'd tried. But I'm sorry. Because I'm beginning to get the picture. One lifetime's not enough. A man wants another chance. And he's not going to get it. Unless he has children. And grandchildren. They're his second chance."

"Romantic drivel," Dave said. "You know damn well you don't regret the way you've lived. All those dewy young girls, one after another. Aside from me and my kind, there isn't a man alive who wouldn't envy you."

His father showed his teeth in what was meant for a vain and lecherous grin. But his eyes were haunted. "Of course. You're right. . . ." He drained his glass and set it on the liquor cabinet and moved for the door. But before he opened it, he turned.

"Now let me ask my brutal question. Why be a middle-aged auntie if you don't want to?"

"Did I say I didn't want to?"

His father blinked at him for a moment, then, with a resigned shrug, turned and walked out.

The girl wore a blue denim dress with a skirt about eight inches long. There was a smudge of ink on her nose. She was no more than a kid but she was the entire office staff of the Provence School of Art at night. Dave had noticed the black-and-white Mondrian front of the school lighted up in the rain as he drove past up Western. And he'd swung into the parking lot. Why? Because you tried everything when you needed a lead in a case. But also because he dreaded going home. The emptiness of the house had hurt last night. Enjoying mourning? Not honestly. The pain was too real. He asked the girl for records dating twenty-six years back. She was making an imitation Aubrey Beardsley drawing, bending over the black counter with the pink tip of her tongue sticking out of a corner of her mouth. She didn't want to be bothered. But when he gave no sign of going away, she sighed and laid down the pen and came from behind the counter and led him down a hall past high rooms where corduroyed youngsters with beards daubed canvases, where a model with flesh like lard sat surrounded by kids charcoaling sheets of newsprint, where a shrill, dumpy, red-haired woman ricocheted instructions off bare walls above the wooden clatter of potter's wheels turned by young bare feet on treadles—led him to a big, still room lined with big, still paintings that were like escaped segments of red-and-white signboards, where a dainty, ravaged old man waved transparent hands at a trio of lean-flanked boys on ladders, who were hanging the pictures.

"Mr. Kohlmeyer," the girl called. "This man wants to see you."

Kohlmeyer did a surprised girl whirl, brows arched, eyes wide, a boy coquette. Except that time had done awful things to this boy. "Yays?" He came toward Dave in his ecru velour shirt and black wide-wale corduroys and his expensive sandals and black dyed hair and mascaraed lashes as if it might be the last walk he would take. Very unsteady. Sick. He dismissed the girl with an embalmed smile. "Thank you, darling." And she went away, with the boys watching her pert little ass.

"This is probably pointless," Dave apologized. "I won't keep you if it is. My name is Brandstetter. I'm a claims investigator for Medallion Life Insurance Company. One of our policyholders has disappeared. I'm trying to locate him, trying to learn all I can about him. He once went to school here. Maybe you can help me."

"Ah? How intriguing." Kohlmeyer was watching the boys again. Not the pictures. The boys. Dave agreed. They were more beautiful. The difference was that the pictures would keep their beauty. Such as it was. The boys would wake up ugly one morning. "What was his name?"

"Olson," Dave said. "Fox Olson."

Kohlmeyer turned so sharply he staggered. "Really?"

"Yes . . . why?"

"Oh . . ." A delicate shrug. "It's only that you're the second person who's come inquiring about him lately. After a lapse of twenty-odd years. Isn't that strange?"

"You remember him?" Dave nodded at the boys hoisting another big canvas into position. "They must come and go. I'd think they'd blur after a while."

"Blur . . ." Kohlmeyer's laugh was a death rattle. "Yes, that's very well put. They do, most of them." He gave Dave a flat meaningful stare. "Even the loveliest."

Dave didn't like being tagged. Not by Kohlmeyer's kind. "Was Olson one of those?" he asked.

"Yes . . ." Kohlmeyer blinked into the past. "Fresh blond skin, lovely mouth, and a simply divine shock of golden hair. The young preferred crew cuts then. Awful. Remember? Not Fox. He anticipated the shaggy sixties." Quick cap-and-bells smile. "No . . . I remember him first because of his very odd name. . . ." Pause.

"And second?" Dave prompted.

"Because he was so *in love*." Kohlmeyer set the two words out like Valentine chocolates from a jar of formaldehyde. "With another boy. I can never remember his name. Something out of Mark Twain."

"Sawyer," Dave said. "Doug Sawyer."

The linered eyes widened. "Why, that's it. How ever did you know that?"

"How did you know they were in love? Any proof?"

The withered mouth turned down, mocking. "Really, does one need proof? The young are so obvious. But, yes. As a matter of fact, quite graphic proof. They spent a summer together at a place called Bell Beach. Some very naked and explicit snapshots resulted. Taken with the aid of a delay mechanism on the shutter. I'd lent it to young Sawyer myself, not knowing, of course, why he wanted it. I found the negatives dangling from clothespins in the school darkroom. Drying. Shocking carelessness. Anyone might have got hold of them."

Dave wondered if he'd given them back, and bet not. For half a dozen reasons, none of them noble. He asked, "Who was it came inquiring about Fox the other day?"

"A public relations man. Big, bluff type. Expensive clothes, but rumpled. The unmade-bed syndrome. It seems Fox has become something of a popular idol in a small way. Radio? Music? I can't recall. . . ." Vague wave of the hand. "This man's been commissioned to do a biography, I told him everything I could remember."

Dave felt cold in the pit of his stomach. "Everything?"

"Well, I assumed anything Fox doesn't like he can always take out of the manuscript." Sardonic smile.

Dave felt sick. "And the pictures? He got those too?"

Kohlmeyer shouted, "No, no!" But not at Dave. At the boys sweating with a gigantic curve of red across white. He tottered toward them. "You've got it upside down."

Dave followed. "He paid you. Right?"

"I'm dying, Mr. Brandstetter. Of cancer." The mouth twitched bleakly. "That can be very expensive . . . Now, if you'll excuse me, I'm pressed for time."

"Just one more thing," Dave said. "The man's name. This writer."

"He introduced himself as Smith," Kohlmeyer said. "But on his check it said Chalmers. Lloyd Chalmers."

Dave came in by the back door and used the extension phone on the kitchen wall. There was no sound in the empty house but the drip of rain from his coat onto the waxed brick floor, while the desk sergeant in Pima connected him to Herrera's home phone. When the police captain picked up the receiver Dave heard television gunshots and the rattle of hoofs. Herrera sounded sore at being interrupted. And he evidently could see the set from where his phone was, because he gave something his attention besides Dave. Until Dave got the story out. Then he said:

"It's wrong. Some kind of lie. Chalmers is a big man, a busy man. He wouldn't go nosing around L.A. for dirt. He'd hire somebody."

"He wouldn't be so big or so busy if he lost the election. And he was losing it. A couple million bucks in building contracts. Junior college. Freeway. It was too important to trust to some slimy professional. What would keep the professional from turning around and blackmailing Chalmers, then, for the way he'd won?"

"Yeah . . ." Herrera didn't like it but he bought it. "Yeah, you put it that way, it makes sense."

"Ask Chalmers," Dave said. "Ask him if he didn't tell Olson to quit the race for mayor or he'd wreck him."

"With some twenty-six-year-old snapshots of a couple teen-age boys blowing each other on a beach?"

"You're a law-enforcement agent," Dave said. "You don't shock. Olson's radio audience would be shocked. Or Olson thought so, which is what matters."

"Shit!" Herrera was unhappy. "Look, I don't see what you expect to get. You want to find Olson. Do you think he'd tell Chalmers where he was going?"

"Maybe Chalmers told him where to go."

"Yeah. To hell." Herrera's laugh was short and not a success. He obviously didn't feel funny. He felt trapped. "Look, Brandstetter, I can't go to a man like Lloyd Chalmers and accuse him of blackmail. He's—he's the mayor of this town, for Christ sake."

"Yeah," Dave said quietly. "Sure. Okay. I'll handle it myself. Tomorrow. I'll bring Kohlmeyer. If he lives. All I ask of you is to be around when Chalmers explains." He hung up.

13

He hung up the wet coat on the dark service porch, mopped up the rain puddle with a big pink cellulose sponge, then made himself a drink, lit a cigarette and stood telling himself he had to eat. He didn't feel like driving to Romano's. Too far in the drizzle. He opened the big copper-toned refrigerator. The white emptiness inside was dazzling. He looked into cupboards. A dusty can of artichoke hearts. He'd shut himself up here too long with his grief. Nothing left to eat. He closed the cupboard.

Behind him a voice said, "There's a place that barbecues chickens on Melrose. You want me to go?"

The only light burning in the kitchen was a dim fluorescent tube over a built-in range deck. An edge of the brick chimney kept it from touching whoever it was who had parted the shutter doors from the dining space. But it was a very young voice. With a trace of Mexican. He knew it.

"Anselmo?" he said.

The boy stepped grinning into the light. Mop of black hair. Face round, brown, smooth as an Aztec pot. Five feet six. Hip-hugger pants of cream corduroy, printed with tiny pink and blue flowers.

Fringed yellow calfskin boots to the knees. Puff-sleeved paisley shirt open damn near to the navel. Single gold crescent earring. Loops of beads. A strong and dusky smell of incense.

"I got my Yamaha outside."

"Your Yamaha will rust," Dave said. "What the hell are you doing here? How did you get in?"

"Madge Dunstan was in the shop today. She told my mom you were making the scene again. I wanted to see you. I been wanting to ever since . . . a long time. I tried to call you at your office but the line was always busy. They said leave a number but I didn't have no number to leave. I was all over. I have this gig, delivering stuff. Then I thought I'll just come here and wait for you. Rod gave me a key one time, you know, to get something for him for the shop—"

"And you forgot to give it back?"

Dark lashes lowered, head lowered, voice lowered. "I didn't exactly forget."

"No? Look, what's this all about, Anselmo? I'm kind of tired tonight." He was. It had been a long, discouraging day. He felt old. Yet now, inside him, something young and very alert got to its feet. He knew why, and was surprised and not pleased. "Some other time?"

"Aw . . ." The black eyes begged. "You got to eat. You're hungry. I'm hungry. I been waiting here a long time. If I get the chicken, we can talk while we eat."

Dave sighed. It was a mistake and he knew it was a mistake but he took bills from his wallet and laid them in the small, brown, not very clean hand. "You win. Get french fries too, and anything else you think might taste good."

"*Sí*. Okay. Ten minutes, I'll be back."

The boots went away soft and quick. The front door closed. Outside, the motorbike spluttered into life and snarled off. Then there was only the whisper of the rain. For a moment Dave frowned at the place where the boy had stood. Then he finished his drink in a long swallow, set the glass down, and began assembling the coffeemaker. . . .

Anselmo's mother had worked for Rod for a long time. A scrawny little woman with a bad temper, who refused to speak English, she could do anything with a power sewing machine. Fast and right. Sometime she'd had a husband. And six kids. All were gone now except Anselmo, a late arrival, his mother old enough to be his grandmother. She brought him with her to the shop, where he would spend the day dressing himself up in scraps of bright cloth. He'd been four, five, six then. Big-eyed, solemn. His mother had rattled Spanish abuse at him when he got underfoot. Rod had ignored him. It wasn't that Rod disliked children. He never saw them. They didn't exist.

In those days, ten, twelve years ago, Dave had enjoyed dropping in at the shop. It was a fine place to be. Rod's ideas had begun to catch on. There was excitement, happiness, promise in the air. There began to be more hired hands too, and Dave had felt sorry for the little kid lost in the turmoil. He'd made it a habit to take him down to the corner for an orange drink or an ice cream bar, to bring him small puzzles in cellophane from supermarket racks, crayons, a coloring book. They became friends.

Then Anselmo started school and they met less often. But now and then Dave would find him at the shop late afternoons. Reading comic books. Dave kept him supplied. On his eighth birthday he took him to a Dodgers game, on his ninth to Disneyland. Then the shop moved to glossy new quarters. Assurance took the place of excitement. Dave stopped going. Now and then Rod spoke of Anselmo. Mostly about trouble between the boy and his mother.

Then he appeared. At a party Rod threw for his staff. At a place with green lawns and a blue pool and low white buildings. Twelve, maybe thirteen, Anselmo had been by then, a dark smudge along his childish upper lip, his voice deepening. He had stuck close by Dave that afternoon. Very close. Dave had all but forgotten. The cabana by the pool. Himself under the shower. The boy lurking by the lockers, staring and pretending not to stare. Meaningless at that age . . .

The Yamaha came back. Dave set the tone arm on Bach partitas played by Glenn Gould and crossed the room and pulled open the front door. Under the wide roof overhang the boy shed a hooded plastic raincoat, draped it across the glinting little machine and came toward Dave, grinning and holding out a wet brown paper sack.

"Thanks. That was quick." Dave turned inside.

Anselmo stopped in the doorway. "My boots are wet."

"Take them off and bring them out here." Dave slid plates from the warming oven. The sack held two small chickens, brown and varnished-looking, swathed in cellophane; a waxed-paper box of french fries; and four soft, leaky little paper cups of orange-colored sauce. He fixed the plates. Anselmo padded in in child-size white gym socks and set the boots by the oven. Dave looked at him. "Does your generation drink beer?"

"My generation smokes grass," Anselmo said. "The table looks nice. Like a picture. What's the music?"

"Would you believe the Rolling Stones?" Dave handed him the plates. "Go sit down. I'll open myself a beer." When he reached the table the boy had a chicken in both hands and half demolished. He grinned at Dave, chewing.

"The Rolling Stones," he scoffed.

Dave smiled, sat down, poured Dos Equis, took a gulp of it and was suddenly hungry. The chicken tasted machine-made. The potatoes were limp and greasy. He had no faith in the Chalmers gambit. He was afraid he'd lost Olson—$150,000 worth. But he ate very nearly as ravenously as Anselmo, who, while he savaged the chicken, watched Dave across the table, steadily, unblinking, with big, dark, liquid, animal eyes. Then the skeletons were on the plates and Dave took them away and came back with coffee, and the boy said:

"I sleep with it under my pillow."

Dave blinked. "What's that?"

"The key. Can I have a cigarette?"

Dave slid the pack to him. "The key to this house? Why?" He lit a match.

"Because you are here." A flush darkened the brown, smooth face as the boy leaned to get the flame. When he sat back his eyes were anxious. "Does that bug you?"

Dave stared. The match burned his fingers. He shook it out. "I . . . guess you'd better explain."

"Do you know what a love-in is? In the park, where the hippies go to do their thing? And they got rock bands make a lot of noise. And people wear"—he glanced down at himself and brought up a small smile—"what they want to. Lots of color. It feels good—"

"It looks good," Dave said, nodding.

"And people give flowers to each other and feed each other and play drums and dance, you know?"

"I've read about it," Dave said.

"And everybody says, 'You're beautiful,' and you say it back. It don't mean how your face is made or like that. It means how you are inside, man, you know? Loving, loving everybody and everything, feeling good about flowers and birds and babies and like that, about everything . . . You understand?"

"I'll have to go to the next one," Dave said.

"No." Anselmo scowled. "No. It's a fake. Don't go. They think all this—what I told you—is the way it is. But it ain't. Oh, maybe for a few people. But mostly they're freaks there. Like fat, pimply girls. They might give you flowers and smile but it's not love-in love they want. They want to be balled. Nobody in their school or anyplace will ball them.

They're too much dogs. They come alone because nobody will bring them. And they tell you, like everybody, 'You're beautiful,' and all that. But if you hang around them, pretty soon they grab your hand and put it under their shirt or up their crotch. It is sad. They don't know nothing about love like what a love-in is supposed to be." He picked up his cup of coffee and set it down again and looked at Dave and said, "You do. You're the only one I know. It's kind. And giving. And it don't try to get nothing."

"The Pauline ideal," Dave said. "You should be a priest, Anselmo."

"Shit," Anselmo said. "They fake it too. I know them. It's money they want. And to run people. Anyway, I like sex. I like it a lot. But not like I've got a faucet and somebody's thirsty so they turn it on and drink and then turn it off and walk away. Like this cat in Venice Beach. I'm down there goofing and he takes me to this pad where they got mattresses and pillows all over the floor and everybody is laying around naked and blowing pot and, like, stroking each other. Real gentle, you know?"

He sat forward and the beads rattled against the table. "*Kerista*, love by touching. It feels good. And everybody there is real cool. Only not me. I'm not hip to the scene. Right away my cock is up. And then he's doing it to me. Well, he's a nice guy. Beautiful. I want to do it to him too. Only he won't let me. So . . . I come and he goes. I went back to Venice four, five times looking for him. Noplace. Then I ran into him in a head shop on Fairfax. He tried to duck out but when he knew I saw him he gave me this shit-eating grin and split. He was with this chick. It made me feel bad. . . .

"Almost as bad as the woman I went with first. My first time. She was on this bus I used to ride home from school, and she had this house and these little kids, and she took me there and laid me. But good. And it went on. And then one time there's this man there when I come. And she runs me off. Says it's her husband. I'm fourteen. I believe her. Then I find out he's just a new stud. She has new studs every couple months. It made me feel bad. . . ."

The music stopped. Dave rose and turned the record. Numbly. He brought coffee from the kitchen, refilled the cups, sat down, gave Anselmo another cigarette, lit it for him, lit one for himself. The boy went on:

"It happens to me all the time. I met this guy on Hollywood Boulevard. Not a kid. A man, like you. Nice. I went with him because I liked him. And afterward, he tried to give me money. Five dollars. Shit!" Despair twisted the childish mouth. "I cry. Every time. Lay on my bed with my face in the pillow and cry like a little kid. And do you know what I keep saying when I'm crying? I never even knew I was doing it at first. 'Dave,' I say, 'Dave.'"

"Anselmo, if this is a put-on . . ." Dave began.

"No!" The boy shouted it, meant it. "I been in love with you from six years old. Sure, I didn't know it was love. I didn't know what it was. Just a feeling like you were the best, you know? The greatest. I used to wait for you to come to the shop. And then after a while you didn't come no more. But I didn't forget. And when Rod threw that party and my mom told me you'd be there, I begged her to take me. To see you. I had to ditch school and she didn't like it. But she let me go because I bugged her so. And then I knew I was in love with you. That day." His eyes were accusing. "I bet you don't even remember."

"I remember," Dave said.

"You took a shower. You were beautiful, naked. I wanted to get in with you." Anselmo shrugged. "I didn't know nothing. Like what to do. I just wanted to be with you and put my arms around you and kiss you. Little-kid stuff. I mean, I was jacking off all the time, by then, but I didn't connect it up. Sex. With love, with what people in love did. Anyway, there was Rod."

"You understood about that?"

"Not too good. My mom told me. She put it pretty vague and I was dumb. I didn't really understand, but I knew you don't bust up somebody's thing, dig? So I just said to myself, 'Forget it,' and looked for somebody else. But they were all bad trips, freak-outs. And I kept remembering you. I couldn't help it. Then Rod gave me the key that time and I came in here. Just walked in. My heart was beating loud and I was shaking, scared. I had it in my head you'd be here. I was like fifteen then and I didn't have no control. It would have been wrong. Because of Rod. I understood by then. But I was out of my head wanting you. It had to happen. Only"—Anselmo laughed at himself, softly—"you weren't here." He watched his small, chicken-greasy fingers turn the cigarette in the ashtray. He shook his head, shamed. "You know what I did? Took off my clothes and got in your bed and pretended you were there. Kids do crazy things."

"One of them is doing a crazy thing right now."

Anselmo didn't hear. "I came back and did it every time I could for a while," he said. "Then—I don't know—it only made me feel worse. But I kept the key. . . ." He drank coffee and set down the cup. "Then Rod died. The funeral was the first time I got to see you in years. You were still very beautiful to me. But you were hurting too bad. I couldn't say nothing to you then. So I waited as long as I could and then I tried to call you but you didn't answer the phone. I came here and knocked but you didn't open up. I used the key. It was very dusty in here. And you were laying on the bed in your clothes and you looked right at me and you didn't even see me. I said hello, or something, and you didn't say nothing. It was scary."

"I don't remember," Dave said, "but I'm sorry."

"No. I was a jerk. I thought I knew what it was to be sad. I didn't know."

"Try not to find out," Dave said.

"But today, when Madge said you were okay and working again and all that, I came back. You got to have somebody." He was solemn. His eyes were wide. "I want it to be me."

Dave drew a deep breath. "How old are you, Anselmo?"

Pride. "I'll be eighteen my next birthday."

"And I'll be forty-five. Look . . . you're very beautiful. You must know that. I want you. You must also know that. But I'm not going to bed with you. Because there's something I know that you don't. It would be another bad trip for you. Maybe the worst."

"Why? You mean because I'm a dumb kid? You'd get tired of me?"

"You'd get tired of me first. My books, my music. And I'm a morose bastard. Rod used to say so. He was right. Find somebody young, Anselmo. If you'll forget me, that won't be so hard. Somebody to keep you laughing and happy, the way you should be at eighteen."

"I won't be happy." The boy stood up, shaking his head. "Not without you. I'd rather have you for just one time than anybody else forever. Because . . . I don't know what is this 'morose,' but you are good and kind and . . . there isn't nobody else like you in the whole world and I've wanted you for . . . all my life. I don't need to laugh a lot. I'll listen to your music. I'll read your books. . . ." He came around the table and stood beside Dave's chair. "I'll do whatever you want."

Dave looked away. "I want you to go home."

"Why? The law? You think I'd fink on you?"

"It never crossed my mind." Dave rose and looked down into the dumb black eyes that would never understand anything he said or did. He wanted to close the hard little body in his arms, to cover with his mouth the boy's mouth, dark, parted, waiting. Younger, he couldn't have stopped himself. He

123

wasn't younger. He said, "I've explained. We wouldn't work out."

Anselmo touched him. "Let's try and see."

"I'm not talking about sex. I'm sure that would be fine. But we can't do that twenty-four hours a day for the rest of our lives. Now, look . . . you said you'd do what I wanted."

The boy dropped his hand. "*Si.* Okay." Mournful, he went to sit on the kitchen floor and pull his boots on. Standing, he gave two little stamps of his feet, like a flamenco dancer. Then he looked at Dave. Gravely. "Only I'm not giving up. Sometime you got to let me. Otherwise there's no point in living."

"You'll find somebody else." Dave steered him to the front door and stood there in the chill breath of the rain, watching the sad pantomime with the plastic coat, the straddling and kicking to life of the Yamaha. The boy rode it away woodenly, eyes front, down the dim street. Crying? Dave shut the door. The music had stopped. The house was very still, very empty again.

In the kitchen, he made himself another drink.

14

He went to bed stoned. But not stoned enough. He
had bad dreams. A giant wasp was trapped in
the kitchen. It buzzed, buzzed, hurled itself
against the fragile shutter doors. He leaned on them,
held them, sweating, horrified. A barbed javelin-size
stinger thrust between the slats. He opened his mouth
to scream for help but no sound came. Then he was
awake and knowing what he heard—the buzz of the
doorbell. Insistent. Under a stubborn thumb. He
staggered to the closet for the blue corduroy bathrobe
and remembered it was still in a grip in the luggage
compartment of the car. He dragged the top blanket
off the bed, wrapped it around him, and stumbled to
the front door and yanked it open.

Maybe it was morning but it still rained and it
was still dark. A big man in a cowboy hat stood
there dripping. Dave didn't know him. But he knew
the little man shivering beside him. Kohlmeyer.
Black eye sockets, white skull face. The big man
moved indoors. He didn't push, didn't touch Dave,
didn't need to. Nobody could have stopped him.
Dave backed. Kohlmeyer faltered in after the big
man and Dave shut the door and switched on a
lamp.

125

"You'd be Lloyd Chalmers," he said.

Chalmers's voice came down like a load of gravel out of one of his big red trucks. "Kohlmeyer tells me he told you a story about me. I want you to know it was a lie."

"But you do know Kohlmeyer," Dave said. "And there'll be a record of the check you gave him. At your bank or somewhere." The thermostat control was on the wall next to the bedroom door. Dave started for it. Chalmers's hand was massive on his arm, hard as concrete.

"Where you going?"

"It's cold in here. I was going to turn on the heat."

"You can go back to bed in a minute," Chalmers grunted. "What I've got to say won't take long."

"But you drove two hundred fifty miles on a rainy night to say it."

"I never said it wasn't important."

"You deny you bought photographs from Kohlmeyer? Dirty photographs of your political rival?"

"Rival, shit!" Chalmers scoffed.

"He was winning," Dave said. "Everybody in Pima told me so. Persuading an opponent to quit a race because of an episode in his past is not an unknown tactic among politicians, Mr. Chalmers."

"I'm not a politician," Chalmers said. "I'm a builder. A businessman. And a good one. The town's kept me in office because they knew I could run things and run things right. Lived in Pima all my life. People know me and trust me. Olson was a jump-up stranger. A clown. They might kid about electing him, but when they got in the polling booth they'd have plunked down their X by Chalmers. Naw. If this idea of yours wasn't so nasty it'd be laughable."

Dave looked at Kohlmeyer. The wrecked little man wore lavender silk pajamas under his topcoat. On his feet, which were blue-veined, thin, and white almost to transparency, were gold-embroidered scarlet Turkish slippers. Soaked. Chalmers had obviously dragged him here straight from bed. Now he racked up a smile. It tried for impudence but the effect was grisly and pathetic. So was the simpering toss of the head. You expected to hear bones rattle.

"The check was for a painting. By a student."

"My wife collects this modernistic junk," Chalmers growled.

"But my story," Kohlmeyer said, "was considerably more amusing, don't you agree?" He winked. It couldn't have been more startling if it had happened in a waxworks. "I fear I have something of an impish quality I've never been quite able to suppress. These fancies spring to mind and"—the narrow shoulders rose, the hands came up and unfolded like diseased petals—"I just blurt them out. I mean, life's so relentlessly *drab*. My little fictions aren't meant to harm—they're meant to *vivify*, is all. I've been called malicious." It hurt him to speak the word. He widened his eyes and blinked. The shutter mechanism was rusty. "I'm not. Truly I'm not. I'm a very *loving* person. Anything I've ever said that's hurt anyone, I've been deeply, deeply sorry for. You must believe that. If I weren't contrite would I have telephoned Mr. Chalmers about this? I mean, the moment you walked out of the door, I realized I'd been elfin again. Pixie, if you please. I flew after you, but you'd gone."

"I'm in the book," Dave said. "You could have phoned."

"I couldn't remember your name. That happens to me now. I'm not old. It's the drugs they give me. For the pain." A tear ran down his face. He did nothing about it. He probably didn't know what it was. "But I had to shrive myself. I couldn't apologize to Olson. You said yourself no one knows where he is. I phoned Mr. Chalmers. Desperately. My dialing finger is a mass of bruises. It took hours to reach him."

"I was at a dinner for the Governor in Fresno," Chalmers said. "Didn't reach home till after eleven. Kohlmeyer was on the phone. I placed who he was talking about."

"How?" Dave asked. "We never met."

"Pima's a small town. I heard about you."

"And what I was after?"

Chalmers snorted. "Proof Fox Olson wasn't dead."

"Is he?" Dave asked. "You didn't have a conversation with him, say on the morning of October eighteenth? You didn't show him some photographs of himself in a homosexual act? You didn't suggest it would be better if he withdrew as a candidate for mayor? You didn't suggest he fake that accident with his car and leave town? For good? You didn't name a place to him where he could drop out of sight?"

Chalmers's face was red. His eyes narrowed. His gravel voice shook. His fists made hammers. "You're damn lucky I brought a witness with me. Because if you were alone here, I'd take you apart so they'd never be able to figure out which piece came from where."

"It's my job to be suspicious," Dave said. "Stop taking it personally."

"I'll take it any God damn way I please."

"If you stood to lose a hundred and fifty thousand dollars," Dave asked, "how genteel would you be about trying to hang onto it?"

Chalmers stared, big jaw thrust out.

"When a man dies," Dave said, "there's evidence—his corpse. A smashed automobile doesn't prove a thing. Olson is alive. But unless I find him, my company's got to pay. Now . . . he disappeared for a reason. I've got a couple of explanations. They haven't led anyplace. I thought Kohlmeyer's might. You'll have to admit it adds up."

"Maybe—to a mind like Kohlmeyer's. I know what's the matter with him. What's the matter with you?" Chalmers reached for the door. "You want to watch who you call a blackmailer." He jerked the door open, pushed Kohlmeyer outside and shot Dave a glare. "I'm not a man to smear, friend. I'm a man to respect and leave alone. Understand me?"

"I was in Pima for two days talking to people," Dave said. "I left you alone. I didn't figure you in this. That was Kohlmeyer's doing. Settle it with him."

"Oh, please . . ." Kohlmeyer fluttered like a tissue-paper kite in the rain. "I'm not a well man. . . ."

Chalmers grunted and slammed the door.

Dave was cold to the bone. A hot shower was what he needed. But there wasn't time. He dressed, wool slacks, flannel shirt, heavy pullover sweater. He lit a cigarette, set the remains of last night's coffee on a burner and dialed Pima's police station. Herrera was going to like being rousted from bed even less than he'd liked missing his Western last night. But it couldn't be helped. Only Herrera wasn't in bed. It was 3:25 A.M. but Herrera was on the job.

"I was going to call you," he said, "soon as I could."

"Look," Dave said, "get to a judge. On the double. Get warrants. Search Lloyd Chalmers's offices—city hall, construction company, home, safe-deposit boxes. He's got those photos. Someplace."

Herrera tried to interrupt.

"He won't interfere. He's out of town. Just left my house. With the guy who sold him the pictures. They claim it was all just a bad joke. There are no pictures. Never were. So why bother to tell me? I wasn't bracing anybody about any pictures. Not yet. Chalmers jumped too soon. He's guilty as hell. Of something."

"It don't matter," Herrera said.

"Maybe not to you," Dave said. "It sure as hell matters to me. Look, it's early. You can do it before anybody in town's awake. Nobody will see you. The mayor will never know. Not if you get a move on—"

Herrera yelled, "Will you shut up a minute?"

"All right," Dave said.

"Thanks. It don't matter about the snapshots. It don't matter about Chalmers. See . . . Olson is dead."

It was like a kick in the stomach. "You mean . . . his body's been found. In the river."

"Not in the river. In a place called Bell Beach, San Diego County. On a broken-down amusement pier. With a bloody hole where his heart used to be. Sheriff's substation there gave us the word. Hour, hour and a half ago. I'd have been in touch with you sooner only I've been on the jump. Carrying the bad news. Up to his wife's, out to his father-in-law's, over to his daughter's. It's the part of this job I hate."

"Let me be sure I understand you," Dave said. "Olson's been murdered? You mean like lately?"

"Last night. Between eight and ten, according to the preliminary medical exam. They'll be more exact about it after an autopsy. Anyway, they didn't find him till midnight. No identification on him, so it took a while to tag him. We heard from them at two."

"Pretty fast work at that," Dave said mechanically. "Who did it—do they know?"

"The guy Olson was sharing a room with there for the past week. He's missing. They've issued an all-points bulletin for him." Herrera's laugh was short. "With ours, that makes two."

"Doug Sawyer," Dave said. "Right?"

Joseph Hansen

"Only not in the Ferrari. Now it's a '54 Chevrolet. About two hundred dollars' worth. You're sharp, Brandstetter. Any time you want a job, you know where to come."

"Thanks." Dave laughed grimly. "I may just have to do that. Soon."

132

15

Bell Beach was lost miles from the freeway. Sand lay in the empty, sun-baked streets. Wiry brown grass thrust through the sand. In the grass, gulls and pelicans stood like moth-eaten museum pieces. The buildings were cheap stucco with mad carnival turrets. Gaudy paint had faded and scabbed off. Shingles had curled and turned black. Windows were broken. Where not broken they were boarded up, had been for years: the rust from nailheads had written long, sad farewells down the salt-silvered planks. The corrugated iron roof of a hot-dog stand had slumped in. A metal filling station turned to black lace in the sun. Beyond padlocked grillwork in a crimson-and-gilt barn shadowy carousel horses kicked through gray curtains of cobweb.

Dave squinted into the sun. Was everyone dead here?

Then out of the sun a fat, leather-skinned old man in ragged shorts and a greasy tam-o'-shanter rode a bicycle. A young Negro in cracked sunglasses lounged against a power pole. Bare torso, Levi's, bare feet. A withered woman in a torn straw hat hobbled out of a grubby grocery store, clutching a sack. Across the street, sitar music droned from a tinny loudspeaker above a shop door. Garish drunken lettering on the windows. A glimpse of beads, books, phosphorescent posters. A squat, swarthy girl with uncombed black hair and a clean new pink-and-orange shift held something shiny to her mouth, blew a stream of bubbles into the air, then disappeared into the dark shop.

Dave braked the car. Down three side streets so far he had seen only blue ocean. This side street sloped to a pier. And on the pier, above the rubble of sideshow booths, rose a massive scaffold, patches of yellowing white paint still clinging to it. At the foot of its steep, rusty tracks, the bulbs had been smashed out of a horseshoe-shaped sign. The sockets spelled THE CHUTE. But they needn't have. Dave would have recognized it from Fox Olson's painting over the fireplace in the canyon house at Pima. He would have recognized it from the sad snapshot of two laughing boys on the seedy counter of Sawyer's pet shop in L.A.

Halfway down the street to the pier, a bright new American flag hung above the doorway of a sprawling stucco monstrosity. Through later coats of paint the old sign high on its side still showed— BELL BEACH BATHHOUSE. But a white enamel sign standing on the sidewalk bore a brown six-pointed star that indicated the sheriff's substation was lost somewhere inside. A dusty estate wagon stood at the curb. Familiar. Dave parked behind it. As he stepped out into the blaze of sun, the door under the flag opened.

Thorne Olson came out. Of course. Herrera had

sent her to identify the body. She wore black. Smart. Her face was tight and she moved fast. She was at the estate wagon and trying to get into it before Hale McNeil had shut the building door. The car door was locked—KPIM on it in green and blue. She turned sharply to McNeil. He unlocked the door. Her gloved hand snatched it open, she started to get in, and saw Dave. Her eyes widened. She poked McNeil, who swung around. Dave walked to them, sand gritting on the cracked cement under his shoes. Closer, he saw what she needed. A drink. She was trembling. But not her voice.

She said flatly, "You were right. You're very clever, aren't you?"

"But not quick," he said. "Not quick enough. I'm sorry. He . . . never mentioned this place to you?"

"No." Bitterly. "It appears there was quite a lot he never mentioned to me."

McNeil put a hand on her arm. He told Dave, "He's dead. Doesn't that close the case as far as you're concerned? What are you doing here?"

Dave didn't know, so he made up a lie. "My company requires its own agent to identify the deceased," he said.

He told the same lie to the deputy in charge of the Bell Beach substation, who was young and trusting. He led Dave along a dingy hall. The building still smelled like a bathhouse—sweat, urine, sodden wood. The door the deputy opened was like a refrigerator door. The room beyond was cold. Zinc counters and set tubs, a drain in the center of the cement floor.

The body that had belonged to Fox Olson lay under a sheet on a high white enamel table. The deputy folded back the sheet from the face. Olson looked young. Death could do that. Erase years. A gull swung between the sun and the windows. Its shadow flickered across Olson's face like a remembered pain.

"Thanks." Dave turned away. "That's him."

"I don't get it." The boy's voice was hurt, disappointed. "Didn't anybody like him?"

"Everybody," Dave said. "Almost. Why?"

"His wife. The big guy—his manager. They didn't bat an eye. They acted like you. Looked at him and said it was him and went away." He hauled open the heavy door.

Dave went through. "They thought he was dead a week ago." He told about the smashed bridge, the smashed Thunderbird. "They've already done their crying."

Though broken up by head-high partitions, the substation was one enormous room. Roman bath style. Flat fluted columns against the walls. High ceiling a pattern of plaster acanthus leaves. Niches for statues. The pool had been floored over. It echoed hollow underfoot. Dave sat in a hard wooden armchair. The deputy sat at a brown steel desk and looked new.

"He couldn't have picked a better place to disappear to. Nobody comes here anymore." His smile was wry. He touched his badge. "That's why we're in charge. Rookies. It's a ghost town. Even the hippies leave. They hear about the cheap rent and how nobody bothers you, and they come. But they don't stay long. It's too dead."

"Yes. What killed it?"

"A coast road used to run through here. State highway, two-lane. They let it fall to pieces when the freeway got built. Nineteen fifty-five. Town went broke. Yup . . . guy wants to disappear, Bell Beach is the place. Nobody'd look for anybody here."

"You included?" Dave nodded at the missing persons dodger with Fox Olson's picture on the desk. "You've had that for days. He must have been around."

"I saw him." Disgusted, the deputy lifted and dropped the paper. "This is what I didn't see. It went in a file. Johnson or Miles put it away. Neither one of them will admit it though. They work the other shifts. I never saw it, I'll tell you that. Not till last night, looking to identify him."

He yawned, blinked, shook his head. "'Scuse me. This is the time I usually sleep. Got to wait for the coroner and stuff . . . Yeah, I saw him. Them. Like on the beach. Umbrella, big towels. They had this ball they'd toss. Swim. Read books. Olson had a guitar. Couple guys on vacation. I even knew where they lived. Old lady Kincaid's.

"But the room didn't tell me anything. Sawyer's stuff was all gone. Olson's was all new. National brands. Nothing distinctive. Nothing you could trace anywhere. Except maybe the typewriter. But I doubt it. Probably paid cash for it someplace, gave a phony name. Mrs. Kincaid had made the rent receipt to

Doug Douglas. She says deceased used the name Edward Fox."

"Edward?"

"That's Olson's first name. His wife told me. Says he never used it. Not even on his voter registration or his automobile operator's license. Noplace but here." The boy yawned again. A groggy smile apologized. "So . . . we had a John Doe. And when you've got a John Doe, you check the files. Take fingerprints, of course. But for news on them you wait—sometimes forever. Meanwhile, you check the files." He fluttered the dodger. His child's mouth went grim. "Hell, if I'd found this earlier, it would have saved his life."

"Maybe," Dave said. "Only maybe. His life had some pretty big rips in it . . . You're sure about Sawyer?"

The boy shrugged. "Who else knew Olson was here?"

"Hippies? Don't some of them have a little problem about what belongs to whom?"

"He wasn't robbed," the deputy said. "Close to four hundred bucks in his pockets when we found him. Cash."

"Have you found the gun?"

"Scuba crew got it out of the water this morning. Fifty feet from the pier."

"Sawyer's?"

"Olson's." He swiveled the chair, opened a file drawer, laid the gun on the desk. A red identification tag dangled from the trigger guard. It was a tidy Colt's .32. "His wife identified it. Also he'd registered it with the L.A. police. Nineteen forty-three. She said he was working in a bookstore on Hollywood Boulevard then. Some GIs held it up. The owner wouldn't buy a gun. Olson bought this. Had it ever since."

"Fingerprints?"

"One. A thumbprint on one of the shells. Olson's. That's all. Gun was oily. Just cleaned before it was fired. Whoever used it wiped it before he threw it off the pier." The deputy held the gun in his clean kid's hand for a moment, tossed it lightly once, then turned and dropped it back into the file drawer. "Look"—he blinked, turning—"have you got some reason to doubt Sawyer killed him?"

"None. It's logical. Maybe inevitable. I'm sorry, that's all. I think Olson had counted on Sawyer to save him. They were old friends."

"They had a fight," the boy said. "A brawl. Mrs. Kincaid heard it. Yelled and swore. Threw stuff. Sawyer took off. This was two, three nights ago."

"He wasn't killed two, three nights ago," Dave said. "He was killed last night."

"Sawyer must have come back. The room was a wreck. And Mrs. Kincaid wasn't home last night."

"Hasn't she any other tenants?"

"Hippies," the deputy snorted. "They were having a party. They had their door shut. Didn't see anybody, didn't hear anything. Making too much noise themselves. Even if they hadn't been, they wouldn't tell me. I'm the fuzz. The man. They won't talk to you unless you've got a beard and your clothes are glued to you with your own dirt and stink."

"The room was a wreck," Dave said, "but Olson wasn't found dead there. He was found dead on the pier."

The deputy nodded. "Under the Chute. But he could have been dragged there."

"At eight, nine, ten o'clock? I know it's a dead town, but that dead? How far is the Kincaid house from the pier? How strong a man is Sawyer? I thought he was slight. If the shooting happened in the room there should have been bloodstains. Were there?"

The boy's face reddened. "No. And Sawyer wasn't any muscle man. And Kincaid's is a good three blocks from the pier. . . ." The boy yawned wide, shut his eyes and let his head hang for a minute. When he looked up his eyes were bloodshot. "I don't know. When we find Sawyer, maybe he'll tell us. . . ."

The door opened. Hot air came in. Also a fat, pasty-faced man carrying a heavy wooden kit by its leather handle.

The deputy stood up. "You the coroner?"

"I'm the autopsy surgeon," the fat man said in a bored voice. "Where is it?"

Dave lifted a hand to the deputy and left.

CONDEMNED. DANGER. NO ADMITTANCE.

The wire-mesh fence slumped as if the signs were too heavy for it. At one point it lay like a rusty circus net. It sprang like a circus net when he stepped across it. In the shadow of the Chute he found the place where Fox Olson had died. Crude chalk outline on the planks. He knelt and stared. Between the slats he saw movement—his shadow on the sun-striped sand below. Pushing to his feet, he dusted his hands. The sand went but not the grease. Black. Automobile grease? He wiped it with his handker-chief, walked to the rail, leaned on it. It left a chalky line across his jacket. He brushed it off. In the stinking dark forest of splintery posts under the pier lay pizza tins, beer cans, cigarette wrappers, condoms—the joyless detritus of American joy. Beneath the spot where Olson had bled was a black splotch. Also a nailhead-size heap of—what? Pale sand? He bent to touch it. Soft. He moistened a finger, picked up a few grains, sniffed it. Sawdust.

Sawdust?

16

The Kincaid house was frame, a big shingle place with cupolas and with fretwork porches all around. It tried to be yellow and managed a sick pale brown. Its unwashed windows stared at the muddy surf across a broken boardwalk and a belt of dirty brown beach. The front door gaped like a senile mouth.

Down the steep porch steps came Hale McNeil, portable-typewriter case in one hand, guitar in the other. The rear of the station wagon was open. Thorne Olson laid clothes inside. Not many. An armload. New sweatshirts, candy-striped swim trunks, chinos, a bright new pair of red tennis shoes.

Dave had left his car at the corner and come walking. She didn't see him until she straightened and stepped aside to let McNeil set what he'd brought inside. Her face was even tighter now, her movements jerkier. Her heels sank in the sand, which didn't help. Then she saw Dave, and before McNeil could stop her, she flared:

"Are you following us? Why don't you leave us alone?"

"Easy," McNeil said, and to Dave, "She's upset."

"I'm not following you," Dave told her. "Remember me? I've been trying to find him. I've got questions.

Now he can't answer them. I thought I'd talk to Mrs. Kincaid." He looked hard at them both. "Or do I have to? Maybe you've got the answers. Why did he leave? Why did he come here? Why was he killed?"

"I don't know, I don't know, I don't know." Shrill, from the raveled edge of hysteria. McNeil's arm went around her. Understandably. She was a widow. He was an old friend. Nothing out of keeping about the gesture. Except that he thought so. He turned color and started to jerk his arm away. No need. She twisted aside, ran for the front of the car, flung herself in and slammed the door.

"It's the sheriff's job," McNeil said. "Why not let him get the answers?"

"Because I don't think he knows the questions," Dave said, and climbed the steps.

Mrs. Kincaid looked like a line backer. Not one who had scrimmaged lately, but still muscular. She wore a one-piece knit swimsuit that looked as if she'd always worn it. The sun had faded it and tanned her until they were the same color. The effect was arresting. She was about sixty-five. She came out of the back of her tousled apartment carrying a battered aluminum coffeepot, and when she saw Dave standing in the doorway of her front room—it was one of those old-fashioned sliding doors and standing open—she gave him a grin that couldn't have been friendlier if she'd had teeth. As a matter of fact, she did have teeth. In a glass someplace. She went and got them.

"There," she said. "Hello. Looking for a room? I got a dandy. Great big. Upstairs at the front. Just vacant though. I haven't had a chance to clean it up yet."

"Fox Olson's room?" Dave asked.

"Oh." She was disappointed. But disappointments weren't new to her. She didn't give this one much time. She was curious. "Who are you?"

Dave told her. "I'd like to see the room."

"I guess it's all right. But look here. . . ." She sat on a humpy old sofa. Books and papers were strewn on the coffee table. She poked among them, hunting something. "His wife just left. She gave me his birth data. I'm an astrologer." She found dime-store reading glasses and began making jottings with a stub of pencil. Her free hand waved toward a banner on the wall.

It was about six feet square and appeared to be painted on heavy oilcloth. MADAME VERA, it said, SEES PAST, PRESENT, FUTURE IN YOUR STARS. The lettering was fancy. It encircled a zodiac chart that held bad drawings of crabs, scorpions, goats and the like. Sometime the banner must have hung outside one of those ruined booths on the pier.

"Look at that," she said.

"I'm looking," Dave said.

"No, no. I mean here. Come on." She slapped the sofa and he sat beside her and bent to look at the paper. Another zodiac chart. No animals this time. Symbols and numbers. "See that? Born with the sun in the eighth house. Bound to die this year or early next. You're in the insurance business.

This is something it'd pay you to know. Eighth house natives die in their forty-fifth year. He had Mars there too. Means death by violence. President Kennedy had the same thing. Funny. Both of them had Saturn in the tenth house too. Downfall from the heights—that's what that means."

Dave said, "Too bad you couldn't have warned him."

"Didn't have his birth data or I could have." She poured coffee into a cracked cup. "Want some?"

It smelled good. He nodded. She hollered from the back of the apartment, "But warning him wouldn't have done any good. Eighth house people carry a heavy load of karma. They don't make their life, their life makes them. Fate." She came back with another cup, this one so chipped the word *shard* would have described it better. But it held the coffee, which was as good as it smelled.

"What do you mean, sun in the eighth house?" Dave asked.

"Anybody born around four in the afternoon."

"Wouldn't that include a lot of people?"

"Very few. Fact. Probably the rarest time of all to be born. See, it's dying time, really. Ask anybody works in a hospital—they'll tell you. Tide goes out, life goes out." The glasses had slipped down to the end of her nose. She took them off. "Astrology calls the eighth the house of death."

"Especially," Dave said, "when something like this happens. Something that fits."

She wasn't hurt. "Astrology's never wrong. It's the astrologers make the mistakes." She cocked her

Joseph Hansen

head. "You're a Venus-Moon type. Not natural for them to be so skeptical."

"It's an occupational disease." Dave set down the cup and stood. "It's upstairs?"

She made a whistling sound in her throat getting up but she did it without hands. "Same room they had before. Summer 1941."

Dave had started to turn. He halted. "You remembered them?"

"Nicest pair of boys ever stayed here. Oh, naturally, I didn't know them right off the bat. It's been twenty-six years. They're men now, not kids. But soon as they says who they were I remembered. They figured I would. Just asked me to keep it a secret." She bent and shut her books and began making a stack of them. "They wanted a couple weeks' peace. Didn't want to see anybody. And would I go along with the gag. Well, naturally, I loved them for remembering me and this place and that summer and coming back. Made me feel real good. I says sure." She straightened. "I'm used to keeping people's secrets. Been doing it all my life."

"Which is why you didn't tell the deputy their real names." Dave grinned. "I'm not surprised they came back here . . . May I see the room?"

"It's awful untidy." She hung back. "See, Fox and Doug had kind of a fight the other night."

"The deputy told me."

"I knew there'd be a cleanup job to do. Broken glass and all that. Doug had left. And when Fox passed my door next morning on his way out someplace— grocery, it turned out—I grabbed the broom and the

146

vacuum and stuff and hiked upstairs to put things in shape. Not right away. Did my own dishes first.

"Well, I'd just walked into the room when Fox comes back. Nothing in the grocery bag that didn't jingle. He tells me, don't bother. Leave it like it is. He wants to write. He looked terrible. Sick and lost and scared. Poor thing. I let him be."

"Then the wreckage the deputy told me about wasn't from last night?"

"No. Room was just like I saw it the morning after the fight." She blinked into the sea glare that came through the front window. "Monday, that was. Fox stayed up there. Ran the typewriter a little. Paced around a lot." She looked at the cracked ceiling. "It's an old place. Floorboards creak. He walked like an animal in a cage. Guess he got pretty drunk too . . . But no, I never did get a chance to clean up the room."

"Then there's no evidence Sawyer came back?"

She scowled. "You mean and killed Fox?"

"Deputy can't figure anybody else doing it."

"He's no more than a baby," Mrs. Kincaid snorted. "If he knew anything about people . . . Of course Doug never killed him. Doug couldn't hurt a fly. It's not in him."

"But you don't know that he didn't come back," Dave said. "You weren't here."

"That's right. Mr. Pickett and I ride up to Encinitas to the picture show. Regular. Every Wednesday night."

"Ride?"

"Bicycles. It's only a few miles. And we've got good

strong headlights. Mr. Pickett got some of those great big red glass reflectors they use on road construction thingamajigs and I sewed them to web belts and we wear them right across our backs. Pick up headlights from two hundred yards. Not that much traffic comes down the coast road at night to see us. Nor in the daytime either. It was letting that road go to ruin that wrecked Bell Beach. Mr. Pickett used to operate the merry-go-round. He thinks Bell Beach can come back. I wish he was right, but I doubt it. Not before us two old fossils are in our graves."

"Mr. Pickett the man in the tam-o'-shanter I saw on a bicycle earlier today?"

She nodded. "Nicest man," she said. "Come on. Fox's wife took his clothes and typewriter and stuff. But that's the only difference. I haven't had the heart to go in there and get it ready, to tell you the truth." She led Dave into the looming, sandy-floored hallway and started up the stairs. "Just haven't had the heart."

The door on the other side of the hall, which faced Mrs. Kincaid's, a sliding door like hers, was open now. The room beyond it was dark. Out of it came running a small sunburned boy about four years old. Naked. He was yelling defiance and running across the porch when a blond girl came after him. She wore a shift made out of ticking. And that appeared to be all. She was thin. A cigarette hung in the corner of her sullen mouth. She caught the baby before it reached the steps, lifted it by one arm and swung it around so it straddled her hip. She toted it back into the dark telling it it had to have its breakfast.

Dave glanced at his watch. It was two in the afternoon. They were at the landing. Mrs. Kincaid saw his gesture. "They stay up late," she said. "Playing drums, tambourines, whistles."

"The baby too?"

"It dances," she said. "They're wild people. Strange. Never used to be anything like that. Do you know what caused it?"

"No. Don't the drums keep you awake?"

"One night. The first. But I been renting rooms to folks for a long time. And a good part of that time I couldn't afford to be choosy. Had to make up my mind to mind my own business and hope the place didn't burn to the ground and that's all. Nobody stays forever. Repair the damage after they've gone. So . . . after this tribe came—that's what they call themselves, you know, a tribe, and sometimes there's twenty of them in there—after they came and drummed and tootled all night, I just said, it's not any noisier than the surf, Vera. You've slept with that for forty years. Go to sleep. And I did. Still do."

They turned to climb the rest of the stairs and over the rail Dave glimpsed a boy with a beard and long tangled hair standing staring up at them. Handsome body, flat as a lath. Wearing only a jockstrap. He didn't react to being seen. He stared into Dave's stare until he got tired, then ambled back into the dark room. Dave caught up with Mrs. Kincaid at the top of the stairs.

17

She was right. The room was untidy. There was a
bay window at the front. A chair had been thrown
through it, a yellow kitchen chair. It lay broken on
the porch roof outside among shattered glass that
glittered in the hard sun. There was glass inside too,
on the scarred floor, on the yarny supermarket throw
rugs. A bottle had been smashed against the yellow
daisy wallpaper and left a runny stain.

Books were strewn around. Their open pages
stirred in the hot draft from the window. So did
papers that had spewed out of a daisy-painted wastebasket with its side kicked in. So did ashes in the
fireplace. An overstuffed chair lay on its back like
a felled rhino. Mrs. Kincaid righted it and yanked
its bleached slipcover straight.

"You can bet that made a thump," she said.
"Thought the roof had fallen in . . . Listen, I been
trying to get my swim for hours now. I realize there's
been a death, and nobody feels worse about it than
I do. He was a sweet boy and just as sweet a man.
Sweeter. Cuts me up he had to come here and die.
Plan was to be happy. And he was happy. Till Doug
left."

Her mouth twisted sadly. She gave her head a

shake. "But . . . life goes on. Has to. I need my swim, I'm used to it. Don't know what you expect to find. That tadpole deputy didn't find anything. But you hang around long's you want." She started for the door. Her rubber go-aheads were held together by grubby strips of adhesive tape. They kicked something that bobbled away like a small brown animal. She picked it up. "I'll say good-bye now, case you're gone when I get back. I don't mean to hurry, pretty day like this."

"If Sawyer didn't kill him," Dave asked, "who did?"

She frowned. "*Forlorn*'s an old-fashioned word. But that's how he was, the little I saw of him, yesterday, day before. Awfully forlorn. Maybe he took his own life."

Dave shook his head. "They found the gun fifty feet from the pier. No fingerprints. You don't shoot yourself through the heart, wipe off the gun, walk to the rail and pitch it into the ocean, go back and lie down and die."

"No . . ." Puzzled, she worried her lower plate around. For a bulldog second it stuck out. Then she popped it back into place and shrugged. "Well, there was bound to be a strangeness. Neptune in the eighth—mystery surrounding the mortality, that's what that means."

"Sure," Dave said. "What about the tribe?"

"Them? Oh, no." She laughed and shook her head. "No, they believe in life. Hate death, hate hurting anybody or anything. That much I do know. They're dirty and noisy and I suppose they smoke that marijuana. And I *know* it's sex, sex, sex, morning, noon and night. They don't care who sees them or much who they do it with. But"—her mouth turned down at the corners—"murder somebody? No."

"How did they get along?"

"With Fox and Doug, you mean? I doubt if they so much as spoke. They've got a saying, you know—never trust anybody over thirty . . . Listen, I'm going to get my swim."

"Sure." Dave smiled. "Thanks. And for the coffee."

She went and he turned off the smile and looked at the desk. It was a stingy kneehole type, bought as unpainted furniture a long time ago and stained and varnished—also a long time ago. A green blotter covered its top. A little copper oilcan had made a circle on it. Next to the oilcan lay a smudged handkerchief wrapped around a slim ballpoint pen. The profile of a little Colt's .32 had soaked into the blotter in oil, looking like a Jasper Johns lithograph.

There was a pint whiskey bottle, empty. A drinking glass, not quite empty. A crumpled Fritos bag. Pencil, felt pen, typewriter eraser, rubber pad the typewriter had sat on. All new. The drawers held a clear plastic pack of pencils, a little red plastic sharpener, a ream of yellow sheets, three hundred sheets of dime-store white in their torn polyethylene bag, a folder of carbon paper, a dollar booklet with seventeen five-cent stamps, and nine cheap envelopes.

Not a typed word, not a written word.

He knelt to examine the wastebasket. Used Kleenex. Pink potato-chip bag, like a collapsed lung. Another empty whiskey pint. The fireplace? Ashes. They had been a thickness of pages. Twenty, thirty? Typed or else why burn them. But they'd been broken up. And the wind kept shuffling the charred fragments. Still, there were experts who could make a lot out of a burned piece of paper. He doubted this case was going to need experts, but he looked around for something to block the fireplace opening.

A big spiral-bound sketch pad leaned against the side of the desk. It swung open when he picked it up. Only one page had been used. On it were half a dozen quick pencil sketches. Slick, professional. A man stripping and putting on swim trunks. The whole sequence. Accurate, wryly affectionate, sad. The man was slight, but unmistakably middle-aged, no boy. Different from the sex photos taken in this same room twenty-six years ago. Dave closed the sketch pad and propped it in front of the fireplace. It almost covered.

He looked in the chest of drawers. Empty. In the closet his foot kicked something that rolled into the dark. He stooped for it. The beachball. A Sav-on Drugstore special. Giddy whorls of color. No clothes in the closet. The bed had been slept on, not in. He dropped the ball on the bed and left the room. Going down the hall, he opened doors. The other rooms smelled hot, shut up. Untenanted. No sheets or blankets on the beds.

The bathroom was at the end of the hall. Old but

shiny, except for a rusty circle at the water level of the toilet bowl and a smear of yellow grease in the washbasin. There was nothing in the wastebasket but a twisted, spent tube of Kip. An ointment for burns. Sunburn? He sniffed the basin. Kip. He stood blinking at it for a minute, then opened the medicine chest. Aspirin and Pepto-Bismol, Merthiolate and an unopened box of Band-Aids.

A tambourine rattled in the hall below. Dave shut the medicine chest. When he reached the top of the stairs, the tribe was leaving. "Can you wait a minute?" he called. "I'd like to talk to you."

They turned and stared at him. The boy had dressed. Khaki shirt with the arms torn off and the tails out. Bell-bottom dungarees. Big blue beads and an iron ankh on a thong. The girl had put on beads too, and had washed her face. It was shiny. Some strands of blond hair had got wet and stuck to her cheeks. The baby had the tambourine. He wore midget Levi's and a little puff-sleeved shirt printed with big purple flowers. There was dried milk on his chin.

"Rap," the boy told Dave in a flat voice. "We'll listen."

"Did you know the men upstairs?"

"Fags," the girl said.

The boy sighed disgust at her. He told Dave, "We didn't know them. One of them split Sunday night. The other one got himself shot last night. That's all we know. Who are you?"

Dave told them. And about Fox's disappearance. The boy's teeth showed in the beard. White teeth.

Big ones. Very straight. "Yeah? Wow, what a trip! Insure yourself, drop out and collect. If he'd stayed alive and you hadn't found him, you'd have had to pay, right?"

Dave smiled. "After some maneuvering."

"How much bread?"

"A hundred and fifty thousand dollars."

"Shit!" The boy laughed. "Shit!"

The baby had been dancing in a circle on the porch, crouched over, rattling the tambourine above his head. He stopped and came back and stood beside his father, giving Dave a steady blue stare.

Dave asked the parents, "You didn't hear anything last night? Douglas—the man who'd left—you didn't see him again? He didn't come back?"

With a twist of smile, the boy put a hand in front of his eyes. "See no evil," he said.

The girl covered her ears. "Hear no evil," she said.

"Speak no evil," the baby said, and put his hand over his mouth.

"You've practiced," Dave said. "I can tell."

"Yeah," the boy said, "but it's our only number. No encore."

And they turned and left.

There was a pay telephone screwed to the wall at the foot of the stairs. The Smithsonian should be told. It had to be the first model after the invention of the dial. But it still worked. A printed label was pasted to its coin box. Emergency numbers. Chipped at by fingernails, but still readable. He rang the sheriff's substation. He wanted the medical examiner. The deputy wasn't the one he had talked to, but he put the fat man on and Dave identified himself. The fat man grunted.

"Two questions," Dave said. "First, were there any burns on the body?"

"Sunburn. Scalp—deceased was going bald—back of the neck, entire back except for the buttocks, backs of the legs, soles of the feet. Not severe."

The tribe had left its door open. Dave could see through the dim room to a bright side window. The roof of a blue car slid past it. He heard the engine, a six with loose tappets. An old car.

"But no burns from fire? Say on the hands?"

"Nothing like that."

"The preliminary . . ." Dave heard the car brake at the back of the house, the engine die. "The preliminary gave the time of death as between eight and ten. . . ." A car door slammed. "Any reason to change that?"

"Contents of the stomach," the fat man droned, "indicate about three hours after eating. . . ." Footsteps thudded on hollow wood. "Officer's report says deceased ate at a café here about six o'clock. Digestive process stopped around nine."

A screen door flapped shut at the rear of the house. A voice called, "Fox? Fox, I'm back." Footsteps came on, running.

"Thanks," Dave told the phone and hung up.

When he turned, a man was racing up the stairs two at a time. Canvas shoes, seedy tweed jacket, a small man, very light build, like a kid, and with a kid's shock of straight brown hair. Like a kid, he grabbed the post at the top of the stairs and pivoted himself toward the front bedroom. Grinning. No kid though. Gray at the temples, gray in a four-day stubble of beard.

Dave sighed and went up after him.

18

He stood bewildered in the middle of the room. The jacket was not American made. Nor the bulky sweater under it. Nor the slacks. They'd all been slept in. On pine needles. He turned, and Dave felt shock in the pit of his stomach. The eyes were shiny opaque, like stones in a stream bed. Rod's eyes. He was the same size and build as Rod, same dark color, same long head. Another man, but like, very like. Even to the voice.

"Who are you?" he asked. "Where's Fox?"

"I've been looking for him for days," Dave said. "My name's Brandstetter. I'm an investigator for the company that insured his life. Medallion."

"Oh . . ." Sawyer said it hollowly.

"And for you," Dave said, "since I learned you were in Pima the night he disappeared."

"Then"—Sawyer's smile was wan—"ze jeeg is op?"

"Or words to that effect. I'd like the answers to a few questions." Dave tilted his head at the bed. "Sit down."

"May I bum a cigarette first? I ran out yesterday. I thought I'd taken plenty, but I smoked more than usual."

158

Dave gave him a cigarette, took one himself, lit both. Sawyer dragged in the smoke gratefully and dropped onto the edge of the bed. Dave sat in the armchair. "Taken plenty where?" he asked.

"The mountains." Sawyer got up, glanced into the closet, came back, sat down. "I needed to think. Hard."

"Which mountains? What town?"

"No town. I kept to back roads. Slept out." He rubbed his stubble. "Water was a problem."

"Wasn't food a problem? Didn't you have to buy gas?"

"No, as a matter of fact." Now Sawyer went to the chest, opened and closed the drawers. "Fox and I had bought a lot of canned stuff. In L.A., when we changed cars. Our original plan was to hole up in Baja. . . ." He knelt to pick up books, shut them, stack them on the chest. "But we'd loved this place as kids, and when we saw how deserted it was, we decided it was safe. We stayed. So . . . the food was still in the car." He came back to the bed and sat down. "Plus extra gas. Two five-gallon cans."

"Then nobody saw you? Not after Sunday night?"

"I passed cars on the road, naturally. Deer hunters were in the woods. I heard them, never saw them. I doubt that they saw me. I certainly didn't speak to anyone."

"Then there's no proof you were where you say you were."

Sawyer blinked worry. "No . . . Should there be?"

Dave got up and walked to the window and stared

159

at the ocean. It was blue here. So was the sky. But fog was building a gray wall at the horizon. He said, "It would help." He turned. "Why did you leave? What was the fight about?"

Sawyer laughed chagrin. "The wreckage makes it look worse than it was. I throw things when I lose my temper."

"It was bad," Dave said, "or you wouldn't have stayed away four days."

Sawyer looked at the floor.

Dave went back and sat down. He said, "Maybe it will be easier for you if I tell you something first. . . ." It was awkward and it hurt. But he told about himself and Rod. All of it, from the beginning in the furniture store, December 1945, to the end in the nightmare hospital, September 1967.

Sawyer stared. "I'm sorry," he said stiffly, "but I don't see what—"

"Oh, come on," Dave said. "A man named Kohlmeyer—what remains of him—has some photographs of you and Fox Olson, made in this room in the summer of 1941."

"Oh . . ." Sawyer breathed.

"It was those photographs Lloyd Chalmers used to drive Olson out of Pima, wasn't it?"

"Yes." Frowning, Sawyer stretched to grind his cigarette out in the china seashell ashtray on the bedside stand. "You could put it that way and be right. But . . ." He shrugged, troubled. "It's not that simple. The photos were a reason to leave, yes. They were also an excuse."

"Because you turned up?"

Sawyer's look was direct. "You've seen those pictures. You know how it was with us."

Dave quoted Anselmo. "Kids do crazy things."

"We meant what we did," Sawyer said gravely.

"Taking pictures of it?" Dave asked.

"Oh, that." Sawyer's laugh was short and rueful. "No, we knew that was a mistake when we went back to the darkroom and the negatives were gone. We were sick. Then Pearl Harbor came and we had other things to worry about."

"What happened?" Dave asked. "Why didn't Fox go?"

"Because we both thought I'd be rejected. I'd had rheumatic fever as a kid. Supposedly my heart was damaged. There was nothing wrong with Fox. But we'd heard the services wouldn't take you if you were homosexual. He told the truth at the induction center and they made him 4-F."

"But they took you."

"Air Force. I deliberately picked them because their physical requirements were the toughest." His mouth tightened at one corner. "I passed with flying colors." He shut his eyes for a second in pained remembrance. "Christ, what a shock!"

"And you didn't see each other again for twenty-five years?"

"Not till I saw his name in the *Times*. Six weeks ago. You see . . ." Pain dulled Sawyer's eyes. "I'd lost my friend. Like you. A French boy. Man. We'd been together . . . almost exactly as long. Since 1945. He was killed in July. He . . ." It was Sawyer's turn to walk to the window. "He was bound to be killed,

of course. He was a racing driver. He'd cracked up a dozen times, spent months in hospitals. So I knew, or thought I knew. But it was bad, all the same." Sawyer sighed, rubbed a hand down over his whiskery face, turned. "I would have stayed in France. But that was over too. They assigned me to England but I didn't want England. Only place to come was home. It was no good. I only sat and stared at television, like a corpse the undertaker's forgotten to pick up. Then . . ." With a wondering smile, he lifted and dropped his hands. "There was Fox. I ran to him."

"You hadn't tried to find him in all those years."

"That's not so," Sawyer said. "When our camp was liberated, in my first letter, I asked my mother. She said she'd lost track of him. He and Thorne couldn't afford a phone so they weren't in the book. And Mom didn't think of the register of voters. My father was dying. She didn't have time to hunt . . . Then I found Jean-Paul." Sawyer came from the window. "I'm sorry, can you spare another smoke?"

Dave handed him the pack and matches. "So what happened when you got to Pima?"

"I phoned the radio station and he was there and he came right over. He walked in the door of that motel room and we looked at each other, and it was as if there hadn't been any years between. Not for me. Not for him, either."

"But," Dave said dryly, "you went back to L.A."

Sawyer narrowed his eyes and studied Dave through the smoke. "You know the answers to all these questions, don't you?"

"Not all," Dave said. "For example—what about Ito, the Japanese houseboy? What happened between him and Fox?"

"Nothing," Sawyer said. "But Fox was afraid it would, afraid he'd make a mistake. He almost did make one that first night. Ito was beautiful."

"I've seen him." Dave nodded. "He was. Is."

"Well, he was standing there naked when Fox went to his room to thank him for making it a good day. That's like Fox. But it was Christmas and he was more than a little smashed. He almost couldn't keep his hands off." Sawyer's smile was thin. "I suppose that's the answer to your other question too—why he sent me back to L.A."

"He'd always fought it?"

"For Thorne. But he hadn't always won. There'd been a couple of sorry little affairs. In the bookstores, after closing. Brief, a night, two nights. Then some boy in the film plant. But they only made things worse. And things didn't need worsening. Those were bad years."

Dave said, "His wife told me."

"She was everything to him. Cheered him on, gave him reasons to work, live, hope. Gave him a child he loved. Finally gave him a career and wealth and popularity and a future like Disneyland." Sawyer shook his head. "And stopped loving him."

"He knew about the affair with Hale McNeil?"

"He found out. Which told him McNeil had only given him the break on his radio station to get next to Thorne. It didn't matter. Fox didn't let it matter. Thorne had wanted this. He owed her for all those years of nothing. And whatever McNeil's motives, Fox couldn't deny the debt. Didn't try. He knocked himself out to make good. For them. Went around grinning, clowning, to show them how happy they'd made him. It began taking more and more booze to make the act convincing. . . ."

Sawyer drove a fist into his palm, rose, walked to the window again. "She'd say, 'You always wanted first editions,' so he'd buy first editions. Fancy microphones, electric typewriters, the kind of piano he'd admired in some store window when they were first married. She'd been eating her heart out for him to have all those shiny symbols of success. That junky, pretentious white car . . ."

Dave squinted. "He didn't want any of it?"

Sawyer swung around. "He wanted one thing. To write great novels."

"Why didn't he do it?" Dave asked. "He had years."

Sawyer shook his head impatiently. "Wasted. Look at it this way. Suppose Dostoevsky had never mentioned his epilepsy, his compulsive gambling. How far would he have gotten?"

Dave said, "He was going to have a book."

"A comic book," Sawyer snorted. "Cartoons and funny sayings. That made him sickest of all."

Dave heard footsteps crunching on the sand outside, the murmur of male voices.

"Then Chalmers came along with those old snapshots."

"To make Fox stop running against him. That was all." Sawyer began carefully breaking slivers of glass from the window frame. "I think he could have. He says he couldn't. Too awkward to explain. That's what I meant by an excuse. To clear out. He was fed up anyway."

"And there was you," Dave said.

Sawyer leaned out the window and dragged in the chair. The leg wasn't broken. It had come out of its socket. He set it on the floor, crouched, and tried fitting it back in. Frowning, he answered, "Yes. There was me." He laid the chair on its side and rammed the leg at the socket. It went in. He stood it up and hammered on the seat with his fist.

Downstairs the tambourine jingled.

Sawyer rocked the chair tentatively, then sat on it. "He called me Wednesday—week ago. I never wanted anything in my life the way I wanted that call. I never expected anything less."

"You were on his mind," Dave said. "You and this place and that summer. He painted a picture of the Chute after he'd seen you. It's hanging over the fireplace in his living room."

"Yes. Coming back here was important to him. To me too. Just to see the place again."

"I think I'd have moved on," Dave said. "Hurriedly."

"We weren't rational." Sawyer shook his head in wry self-disgust. "Forty-four years old and like a couple of moonstruck adolescents. Wonderful! He was going to write. Did write. Honestly, at last. I . . . was going to paint again. Most of all, we were going to love each other. That went without saying. . . ." He leaned forward, elbows on knees, hands hanging, head drooping. "And that was the part that didn't work. Twenty-five years is a long time. Fox . . . was like a man starved. It was all right at first. Fine. But—well, by Sunday night, I'd had it. I'm okay now. We can talk it out. We will. Because it's worth it." He got off the chair. "Only now I've got to find him. Don't know where he could have gone. He didn't have a cent of money."

"You better sit down," Dave said. "I've got bad news."

But footsteps were coming up the stairs and Sawyer was at the room door in three strides with the expectant grin on his face again. He stopped, gripping the doorframe. Behind him, Dave stopped too. At the top of the stairs stood two young deputies in crisp tan uniforms. They looked big-eyed, like children sent alone to the barber for the first time. One of them started to speak and cleared his throat and started again.

"Douglas Sawyer?"

"Yes?"

"I have a warrant for your arrest." A scared hand brought it out of a breast pocket. "You have the right to remain silent. If you give up that right, anything you say can and will be used against you in a court of law." The boy's forehead furrowed in the effort to remember the long speech. "You have the right to speak to an attorney and to have an attorney present when we question you. If you desire an attorney and cannot afford one, an attorney will be appointed without cost to you, before questioning."

"For what?" Sawyer asked. "Arrest for what?"

"The murder of Edward Fox Olson," the boy said. "On the evening of Wednesday, October twenty-fifth."

Dave saw Sawyer's knees give for an instant, then straighten. He swung toward Dave. Under the stubble, his face was the color of pale clay. The eyes accused.

"You knew," he said.

"I'll get you a lawyer," Dave said.

The deputies clinked when they moved. They handcuffed Sawyer's wrists behind his back, took his arms, turned him and went down the stairs with him, one on each side.

At the foot of the stairs the bearded boy, the blond girl and the baby with the tambourine stared. The baby had stuck something into his mouth like a cork, the small, brown something Mrs. Kincaid had picked up off the floor of Fox Olson's room half an hour ago. Dave knew now what it was. The rubber tip for a cane. He went down to get it.

19

In the glass-and-steel box of the Signal station they looked like school pageant chrysanthemums. Their hair. Hers yellow white, his yellow orange. Shag heads. They sat in the 150-watt glare at ten-thirty at night and stared at each other, with nothing flowerlike in their child faces. Grief in hers, sullenness in his. And fear when they turned to see Dave in the doorway. The boy stood up. Fast.

"Gas?" he said. "You want gas?"

"It's Mr. Brandstetter." The girl tried to smile.

The boy tried to edge past Dave. "Regular or ethyl?"

Dave stood in his way. "In a minute. First I'd like to hear about the letter."

Under his freckles the boy's skin went green. The girl jerked to her feet. The tin chair she'd sat on hit a tin shelf of quart motor oil cans. They fell with heavy liquid thuds like tabla. They rolled on the green cement.

"Wh-what letter? I don't understand." It was unrehearsed and badly delivered.

"From Fox Olson," Dave said.

"He's dead," Sandy said.

"He wasn't dead when he mailed it. Monday

night, Tuesday morning. He was alive, in a town called Bell Beach, five hours down the coast from here. He was alive Wednesday when"—Dave looked at the girl, who had stooped and was groping after the scattered oil cans, her eyes fixed scared and blue on Dave—"you opened it. No, I don't think it was addressed to you. I think it was addressed to Thorne Olson."

"I open all the mail," she said defensively. "It's part of my job. This letter looked—"

Sandy made a sound and lunged at her. Dave caught his arm and twisted it behind his back.

"Easy," he said. "Don't blame this on her. Blame it on your own bad grooming. A gentleman cleans and polishes his boots before going places with a lady."

The boy stared down at his shoes. Clumsy high tops. Old. Caked with black grease.

"You left tracks," Dave said. "Beside the body. Fox Olson's murdered body. On the pier at Bell Beach."

"I didn't kill him." Sandy tried to wrench free. "He was dead when we got there. His room was empty. Something burning in the fireplace. Piece of paper tacked to his door. 'On the pier,' it said. So we went to the pier. He was there. But he was dead. Blood all over the front of him. Somebody shot him in the chest. Not me. I don't even own a gun. I hated his guts but . . . I wouldn't do that to him. I wouldn't do it to anybody."

"It's true." Terry nodded. Tears started down her face. Her voice was a small, thin, kindergarten wail.

"He was dead. All the jokes and the songs, all the kindness and—" The cans rolled out of her hands. She crouched in a corner of the green sheet-metal wall and sobbed. Heartbroken. The word was no good anymore. The trouble was, nobody had invented a better one.

Dave let the boy go. "What was in the letter?"

"I never saw it." He stared miserably at the girl, rubbing the arm Dave had twisted. "She just said he needed her. She had to go to him. Her car wouldn't make it. Mine would. Please would I take her? So"—he grimaced—"I took her. Terry . . ." He knelt by the girl and stroked her shoulder clumsily. "Baby, don't."

"Then she'd given the letter to Mrs. Olson?"

The boy nodded without looking up. "With the rest of the mail. They still get bags full."

"Why didn't you go to the sheriff in Bell Beach?"

The boy's glance was disgusted. "What for? I didn't know who killed him. They could decide I did it. I never kept it a secret I hated his guts. Jesus—the way the people around here *loved* him! Sickening." Short sour laugh. "He was *queer*. Did you know that? Said so in this letter."

"See?" Dave said. "He wasn't after your girl."

Sandy's look was bleak. "No, but she was after him. Crazy about him. Even when she found out he was a flit."

A tote bag sat on the desk. Bright yellow canvas with a white Japanese symbol on it and white cotton rope handles. Girl things inside. Dave set it in front of her. "Come on, Terry," he said, and to Sandy, "Lock up. We'll take my car."

The boy straightened. Slowly. Wary. "Where to?"

"You discovered the body." Dave helped Terry to her feet. Shaky, still whimpering, face wet, nose runny, she poked in the tote bag for Kleenex. "That makes you witnesses. If you're lucky, the Pima police will take your depositions."

"Yeah, lucky," Sandy said.

"Look at it this way," Dave said. "It saves you another trip to Bell Beach. For the inquest. Down and back. That's fifteen dollars' worth of gas."

He left them with a fat young sergeant and a stringy, painted woman who ran a stenotype machine. He went to look for coffee. He found Herrera, red-eyed, unshaven, tie loosened, collar unbuttoned. His ashtray was crammed with the black stubs of cigarillos. Another stub smoldered in the corner of his mouth. He squinted against the smoke and shuffled papers. A lot of papers.

"What rank do you have to make before they let you sleep?" Dave asked.

"They don't have a rank like that," Herrera said. "Not on a homicide."

"I thought that was San Diego County's worry."

"Huh?" Herrera scowled. "Oh, you mean Olson. Forget that." He picked up a stained styrofoam cup. Empty. "We got our own now. Had it since nine this morning." He pinched out the inch of cigarillo and tried his pocket for another. The pack was empty. He crumpled it and slammed it into the brown metal wastebasket. Also the empty cup. Dave gave him a cigarette. When he had the light, he sat back in the leather swivel chair and blew smoke through his nose. "Yup. When his secretary walked into the office this morning, our distinguished mayor was at his desk as usual. Just one little upsetting detail. Half his head was blown off. With a shotgun."

Dave winced. "Chalmers?"

"Lab says he'd been there maybe two hours. Only man in the building then was the janitor. Old guy. Deaf. He thought he heard a noise. Went to look at the boiler in the basement. Never looked anywhere else. Seven-ten. Chalmers just about had time to get back here from your place in L.A. and he was dead. Shotgun," Herrera repeated bitterly. "Most anonymous weapon in the world. Must be a thousand of them in this valley." He got up, headed for the door. "You want coffee?" Dave said yes and Herrera put his head into the hall and shouted, "Any more poison in that acid vat?" Someone yelped an answer. Herrera came back. "One thing will interest you. . . ." Less tired, he would have sounded smug. "No dirty pictures of Fox Olson and his high-school buddy. Nowhere. We've looked at every piece of paper Lloyd Chalmers owned. . . ."

The old man could have been a propped corpse. He sat on the edge of his bed in pajamas and a green flannel bathrobe so new the cuff still had the price tag. The Mexican woman stood beside him in a flowered quilted housecoat. She bulged inside it like steel springs. Her hair was in two thick dark braids for the night. Her eyes were large and brown and watchful. The old man's eyes had a glitter. It was all that told he was alive.

Dave held the little brown rubber cup out to him. "This is how I know," he said. "This was in his room at Bell Beach."

The old man's cane leaned against a straight chair that his clothes hung over. Not neatly. Things had spilled out of the pockets onto the waxed tile floor. There was no rubber tip on the cane.

"All right," Loomis croaked. "I was there. That don't prove I killed him. He wrote me a letter. Says where he is. Says if—" He broke off. "Don't matter what he says. I went. Old place on the seashore. He set there at the desk in that room, stuff all strewn around ever which way, cleaning that little six-shooter. He looked bad. We talked. I come away. I never killed him."

"What did you talk about?" Dave asked.

Loomis's bony shoulders lifted. "One thing another."

"I think he told you why he left Pima," Dave said. "I think he wanted to come back."

Loomis studied his bony feet. The bed was high. He swung the feet a little. It didn't remind you of a child. It reminded you of an anatomy class skeleton. When he looked up there were tears in his eyes and a break in his voice. "Yup. And I wouldn't let him. Says stay away. You come back and you'll wreck Thorne's life and Gretchen's life. Everything. My life." He laughed at that bleakly. "I took cash with me. All I had in the house. Near four hundred dollars. I give it to him. Says I'll send you more. Regular. Not checks. Money. You keep hid. Keep moving . . . I liked the boy. A whole hell of a lot, tell you the honest truth. But . . ." He looked at the swaying skeleton feet again. "What in the world could a body do?"

Dave knelt to fit the tip on the cane. Under the chair lay an envelope. Black-and-white Mondrian design in the upper-left-hand corner. *The Provence School of Art.* He picked it up. He stood up. To the Mexican woman he said, "*Señora. Salga nos, por favor. Un poco tiempo.*" She looked doubtfully to the old man and he nodded and she went, shutting the door. Dave told Loomis, "I think you knew what to do."

The old man's mouth gave a hopeless twist. "Not till too late." He didn't look at Dave. He looked at the envelope. It was turning brown at the edges. It had a dusty feel. Inside were twelve glossy photographs. Fox Olson and Doug Sawyer, naked and young, laughing and sex up, in the daisy-papered second-story-front room of Vera Kincaid's Bell Beach rooming house, summer, 1941. Dave sat on the chair and began tearing them up, one by one, into small pieces. "Not till too late," the old man said again. "Not till Herrera come and told me he was dead. Then I went to do what Fox should have done in the first place. Chalmers's car was gone. I waited. Hours. Not where anybody'd see me. Trees and brush along his private road. Stopped him on the road. He's big and tough. I'm half dead. But a shotgun's an equalizer. I told him flat I was going to kill him. He thought I never meant it. Thought the pictures was all I wanted. They wasn't. I meant it."

Dave stood up. "Bathroom?" Loomis nodded at a door and Dave walked into a glaring green mosque and turned the envelope upside down and watched the fragments shower into the toilet. He made fragments of the envelope and dropped those too. He flushed the toilet and went back. Loomis didn't look at him. He lay on the bed now, staring at the ceiling, seeing something nobody else could see. "Not till too late," he said again.

The shotgun was on its rack in the bare white office. Dave reached for it and the Mexican woman said behind him, "It is clean, *Señor*. I cleaned it myself."

20

When she opened the door her face looked young and flushed. Loved. Her eyes were brandied. He didn't give her time to say anything. He walked past her into the long, raftered room. The only light came from a fire dying in the grate. It was enough to show him that the painting of the Chute was gone. The coffee table had been pushed aside. Two snifters glinted on the hearth with the bottle. Cushions were on the deep rug. So was the black Mexican ashtray. Two brands of filter cigarette had been stubbed out in it. Gauze was wrapped around her hands.

"I didn't see that this morning," he said. "You were wearing gloves."

"I'm not very clever in the kitchen," she said. "What do you want? It's after midnight. If there are papers I have to sign, I should think they could wait till morning."

"It didn't happen in the kitchen," he said. "It happened in your husband's room at Bell Beach. You burned the pages of a novel he'd written there. Which seems a little odd, after the way you've hung onto all the others."

"She didn't burn it." Hale McNeil came out of the dark, tucking in the tail of an expensive wool shirt. "She burned herself trying to rescue it. I burned it. It was disgusting. The whole filthy episode is disgusting and I don't know why you can't leave it alone."

"When you took the typewriter this morning," Dave said, "you ought to have taken the rest of the stuff, emptied the desk. Then I'd be leaving it alone. I'd agree with the deputy in Bell Beach, that only one man knew where he was, therefore that man had to be the one who killed him. But those envelopes were there. Nine of them. The kind you buy at your neighborhood friendly. In packs of a dozen. A dollar booklet holds twenty stamps. This one had only seventeen. So he'd mailed three letters. With Bell Beach postmarks. Which meant that not just one man knew he was there. That's why I can't leave it alone."

"He was writing a novel," McNeil said. "Why weren't those letters to publishers?"

"I don't know why, but they weren't." Dave looked at Thorne. "One was to you. Terry not only opened it, she read it."

"Oh, no!" Thorne whispered.

"That little bitch!" McNeil snarled. "All right. So Thorne got a letter from him. What does that prove? It was a pretty sad document, I'll say that. Apology. Panic. Self-pity. His boyfriend had run out on him. He was all alone. The walls were closing in. What was he going to do? Didn't anybody care? Help, help, help!"

"Hale, stop it!" Thorne was white.

"Sorry." McNeil turned away. "But they're all

alike. I know. I had one for a son." He picked up a wedge of eucalyptus trunk and laid it on the fire. The tattered bark sputtered. "Very nice and charming. Sweet guys. Till they get themselves into some loathsome scrape. Then they fall apart. And the people they've betrayed are expected to pick up the pieces."

"Is that why you went to Bell Beach last night?"

"You mean this morning." McNeil jabbed at the log with the poker. "When Captain Herrera came and told Thorne he was dead." McNeil set the poker in the rack and walked into the shadows talking. "She telephoned me. We went together." He came back with another snifter. He poured into all three. "This morning. You saw us."

"And I acted badly," Thorne said, "and I'm sorry. But the letter wasn't like that." She sat small in a corner of the couch, feet tucked up, facing the fire. "It wasn't a whine. The typing was bad. I think he was drunk when he wrote it but it wasn't a whine. I wish I had it to show you. I don't. Hale burned that too." Her look was unforgiving when McNeil handed her brandy. "It was the saddest thing you ever read. Did you know . . . everything I bragged so to you about the other day, all of it, all the bright, shiny success—he didn't want it? He was just trying to please me."

"I've talked to Sawyer." Dave took his drink from McNeil and sat down. "He said something about it."

Thorne's mouth went bitter in the firelight. "Of course. He would have told *him*."

Fadeout

"He was too decent to tell you. Till it was over."

McNeil sat cross-legged on the hearth, big, handsome, assured. "Decent?" he scoffed.

"Damn decent. And a lot of other old-fashioned words. Kind. Faithful." They didn't like that one. So he told them the Ito incident. "And it was the same when Doug Sawyer came. Sawyer wanted him. He wanted Sawyer. But he sent him away. For you. Both of you. Even knowing what was going on between you . . . It's rude as hell, but we all know manners aren't what they once were . . . Why, when everything was coming your way, when everything you'd dreamed of for him came true—why did you stop with him?"

"It is rude," Thorne said. "But at least you care, which is more than he did. Or seemed to." She got up from the couch, walked to the edge of the firelight and stood gazing down the room to where the flames were reflected in the glass doors to the patio. She said, as if reciting something long memorized, "He needed me. All those years. Trying and trying and getting nowhere. He needed me. Then . . . he didn't need me anymore." She gave a sad shrug.

"Some marriages," Dave said, "should be called on account of darkness."

"That's very clever." She came back into the light. "And very true. I thought I was making him happy. He thought he was making me happy. And we were both wrong." She blinked into the fire. "Neither of us got what we wanted. Not for each other. Not for ourselves."

"Oh, I don't know," Dave said. "You got McNeil."

She turned sharply, stung. "He got Doug Sawyer."

"Not soon," Dave said. "And not for long."

"For a lifetime," she snapped. "Not that I was bright enough to realize it." Her laugh had a rusty edge. "Twenty-four years and I never understood. The shine in his eyes when he used to talk about him . . . Of course he was in love with him. Had been long before I met him. Would be forever." The hurt was still new, still raw. She dropped down by McNeil. His arm went around her. He drew her head against his chest, stroked her hair. She gave a long trembling sigh. "How good it is not to have to be the strong one anymore."

"They're all alike," McNeil said. "No guts."

"I'm sorry about your bad luck with your son," Dave said. "But you don't want to let it short-circuit your brain. Olson had guts."

"Not enough to knock Chalmers down and take those pictures away from him."

"Knocking people down doesn't occur to everybody as a way of solving problems."

"It doesn't occur to faggots," McNeil said.

"I can name you a welterweight faggot who beat an opponent to death in the ring a couple of years ago . . . But I'm interested in your philosophy. Does it extend to guns? Are they another problem-solving device you endorse?"

McNeil's eyes narrowed. "What the hell do you mean?"

Dave tilted the little globe, watching the brandy swirl in the red firelight. "Say the little .32 Fox Olson was cleaning when you got to his room last night."

McNeil started to get up.

"No . . ." Thorne's bandaged hand stopped him. "He wasn't cleaning the gun. He wasn't there. No one was. The door was standing open. It was the loneliest-looking place I ever saw. He'd tacked a note to the door. Felt pen on yellow paper."

Dave nodded. "'On the pier.' Right?"

She frowned. "Yes. How . . . did you know?"

"Terry saw it. And her boyfriend. She made him drive her to Bell Beach. I take it he couldn't leave until his shift was up. They got there after you. The papers were still smoking. When did you leave here?"

She grimaced. "I . . . hate the mail. Fox loved it, adored all those funny little people with their grubby little pencils."

"Pretended to," McNeil growled.

"Yes . . . that's right—pretended to." She gave a wan headshake. "Anyway, I didn't want to face it. And I found other things to do. Nothing things. For hours. Finally, long after Terry left, I went out and tackled it. But it was three by the time I found Fox's letter. Since it was addressed to me, I should have guessed Terry had been up to something. She normally sets my mail aside. This was in with all the fan mail." Her mouth made a thin, pained line. "God, when will it ever stop?"

"I wouldn't have gone," McNeil said. "He was drunk when he wrote it. He was probably already sorry he had. But Thorne insisted."

"So you left when?" Dave asked. "It was before four. I tried to telephone you then. From Los

Angeles. About something that doesn't matter anymore."

"Ten minutes to four," McNeil said. "But I fouled up the detail. Drove a good twenty miles past it on the freeway. Had to backtrack. Must have been nine-thirty by the time we got there. Hell of a place to find."

"A lot of people found it," Dave said.

"And so there was the note," Thorne said. "And we went out on the pier. And he was there. . . ." Her voice wobbled. She got up and went quickly into the dark. "Dead."

"Under the Chute." Dave tilted his head at the blank chimney facing. "What happened to it, by the way?" He raised eyebrows at McNeil. "Your incendiary propensities at work again?"

"If you mean did I burn it"—McNeil scowled—"hell, yes, I burned it. Why should she be reminded?"

"It was a good painting," Dave said.

"Not when you knew what it meant."

"Yup." Dave set down the brandy. It didn't taste good anymore. "So you left him lying there. Right? He was great, wasn't he, as long as he was making a mint for you? He was great to be so obliging about his wife—" A sharp sound came from Thorne somewhere. "But when he turned out to be queer, and a murdered queer at that, very possibly murdered by another queer . . . then he wasn't a friend anymore, a husband anymore. He was just another corpse, like some dead wino in a skid-row doorway."

"That was what he wanted," McNeil said

stubbornly. "That was why he left Pima—to protect Thorne and the rest of us. You don't know what a scandal like that can mean. I do. The one over Tad killed my father . . . We didn't have any choice. We had to leave him there. To have gone to the authorities would have canceled out what he himself did, made it worthless, meaningless."

"Neat." Dave stood. "All right. You live with it. I'm glad I don't have to." He headed for the hall, the way out. Thorne stood there in the dark, hunched, miserable.

"There'll be a scandal anyway," she said tonelessly.

"Just one nice thing," Dave said. "It can't hurt Fox Olson. Not now."

He went out and shut the door.

21

The shack slept under its ragged walnut trees. He put the car where he had put it last time. He climbed the broken stoop again and rapped the new aluminum screen door. But no light went on. Nobody came. In the weeds ten acres of crickets sang. The sky was the scoured black of an iron frying pan, with stars like spilled salt. He knocked again. Waited. Nothing. Frowning, he opened the screen and tried the warped door. Locked. He left the stoop then and, stumbling on rutted ground, walked around the shack. The kitchen door was locked too. But from a window at the far back yellow light poured. Buddy's window? He found a weathered orange crate and stood on it.

The boy sat in the shiny wheelchair. Still dressed. His face was white with tiredness. Dave rapped the glass. The beautiful head came around in an agonized twist and after a blank second a smile of recognition worked the mouth. But the rain-colored eyes didn't smile. They were frantic. The window lacked half an inch of being shut. Dave wedged his fingers under. It went up easily but started down again right away, shuddering in the crooked frame. It made climbing through awkward. His knee toppled a stack of paperback books.

"What goes on? I thought your bedtime was nine."

"It is. Look . . . can I ask you . . ." The young face colored. "I . . . need to go to . . ."

"The bathroom," Dave said. "Sure."

He pushed the wheelchair. When he had the boy set on the fixture, he went through the house. Angry, moving fast. In the front room he found Mildred Mundy. She was sprawled face down on the sofa in her pink kimono. A wine bottle had dropped from her puffy fingers. It lay on the braided rug. Some of the contents had spilled. The room stank of muscatel. He shook her. The loose flesh shuddered but the bloated face was inert. Saliva ran from a corner of her mouth. She wouldn't be any good—not for hours. The television was on. No sound. Just the picture. An old gangster movie. He shut it off and returned to the bathroom. Getting the pants back up the sad useless little legs, setting the boy back in the wheelchair, he grated:

"Where the hell is your brother? Where's Gretchen? How could they do this to you?"

"Gretchen didn't . . . know . . . Mama had . . . mon . . . ey for wine. If she . . . does . . . n't . . . have wine . . . she's all . . . right."

Dave found pajamas on a hook on the inside of the closet door. He laid them on the bed and began helping Buddy off with his sweatshirt. This wasn't the bright-red company one. This one was gray, much washed, much mended. Getting it off wasn't easy. But they managed. Getting the pajama top on was even harder. But the boy was stoic with the spindly arms that wouldn't move where he asked them to, the shining head that refused to hold still on its frail childish neck. And if Buddy had the patience for a lifetime of this, Dave had it for one night. The pajama pants were easier. And there was no problem about lifting him into bed. He weighed next to nothing.

In the time it took, Dave learned that Mama got the money for wine in nickels and pennies from the grocery change. Phil and Gretchen both worked. They had to let her do at least some of the shopping. She hid the coins sly places until she had sixty-nine cents. Then, when they turned their backs, she got her bottle. Once she had it, you couldn't take it away from her. The times they'd tried, she'd been too terrible. Broke things, burned things. You had to let her drink it. But . . . she didn't always drink. Only sometimes. When she was upset.

"What's upset her now? Fox Olson's death?" He said it harshly and wished he hadn't because it made the boy close his eyes as if he'd been slapped. But they were clear when he opened them. He knew how to handle hurt.

"No," he said. "Some . . . thing's wr . . . ong with Phil." Phil had been tense, worried, not eating. Short-tempered too. He'd sworn at his mother, snarled at Buddy, slapped Gretchen. Maybe it was a good thing he wasn't home much. He waited for the mail each morning. "He's ex . . . pecting some . . . thing that . . . does . . . n't come."

"It will be addressed to Gretchen when it does," Dave said grimly.

"You mean," Buddy asked, "Fox's . . . life in . . . surance?"

Dave nodded. "Go on. What happens after the mail?"

"He works . . . at Chal . . . mers Con . . . struc . . . tion Company." There was pride in Buddy's eyes. "He's the . . . chief ac . . . count . . . ant." After five he went to the apartment he was building. He worked every evening there. And weekends. Last night he hadn't come home till two. That was why Gretchen wasn't here now. She said he was making himself sick with overwork. She'd gone to get him, make him come home. "But that . . . was hours . . . ago."

The sheet was clean but tired and patched. The blankets were thin cotton. He tucked them around the boy's shoulders. The cheap metal reflector lamp stood on the worktable shining on a plastic hot-rod model only partly assembled. Dave turned off the lamp.

"Where is this apartment?"

"Ar . . . royo Str . . . eet. Two elev . . . en."

"Thanks. You want this door open or shut?"

"Shut, pl . . . ease." But would Dave leave the bathroom light on and the door open? Sometimes Mama needed it in the night. She got sick. "But . . . this morn . . . ing it was Phil. When the news . . . came on the tele . . . vision . . . that Mr. Chal . . . mers was dead . . . Phil got ver . . . y . . . sick."

Arroyo Street was an unlighted strip of blacktop between orange groves, the trees sprawling, neglected. At places they'd been bulldozed out to make lots for houses not yet built. There were no sidewalks. Brush edged the tarmac. At crossroads, clumps of eucalyptus towered, shaggy black against the sky. Not much farther and Arroyo Street would end. At the river. He slowed to turn around. Then he saw the apartment.

Raw new, two-story, wrapped in tar paper and chicken wire, it was scaffolded around by two-by-fours and planks. A hot naked worklight hung from a rafter end at a corner of the roof. It glared on Phil Mundy. Stripped to the waist, slick with sweat, he troweled and spread green stucco. Relentless, desperate. The scaffold shuddered. Below him on ground littered with lumber scraps, sand, bent nails and sawdust, a noisy one-cylinder gas motor turned the dribbling barrel of a mixer. Frail and incongruous in a mini-dress with swirls of bright color, Gretchen hauled a heavy bucket up a ladder.

"Phil," she shouted above the pop and splutter of the mixer, "please, Phil, I can't. I just can't. You've got to quit now. You can't do it all."

He heard her but he didn't pay any attention. Blank-eyed, completely self-absorbed, he knelt and reached down and grabbed the full bucket by its handle and pushed an empty one at her and got up and swung at the wall again. She came down drooping, head hanging, and stumbled toward the mixer. Dave went to her.

"Did you get a letter from your father? Wednesday morning?"

She was too tired to be startled. Her eyes were

dull. She shook her head numbly. She said, "Have you brought the insurance check? Fox is dead now. You know that." She looked up at Phil, squinting her eyes against the blaze of light.

The bright torso moved, stooped, straightened, swung. The stucco grated under the trowel. Green blotted out the tar paper in wide, curved swaths. Like a flag of truce, a shirt hung from the scaffold. Dave looked around for a jacket. It was hunched on a handle of an upended wheelbarrow. There was a dim, chalky line across its front. He said to Gretchen:

"You'd better go home. Your mother-in-law's passed out, courtesy Gallo Brothers. Someone should be there with Buddy."

"Oh, God." She picked up a flame-colored coat from a sawhorse. "Thanks. How did you know?"

"I'm tracing some letters your father wrote. Your mother got one. Hap Loomis got one. I thought you might have. I went to your house to ask." He told her what he'd found. "Go along. I'll talk Phil down."

Her smile was hopeless. "You're a nice man, but I doubt you can do that. Not without the check. I . . ." The smile died completely. "I'm afraid he's . . . like, cracking up, Mr. Brandstetter. I'm kind of frightened."

"Is he trying to finish the place single-handed?"

"He had to let the crew go. No money to pay them. Oh, he kept one man. But he won't work twenty-four hours a day. Phil's trying. But it's killing him. He was white as a ghost when he got home last night. Two A.M. Just before"—she looked away into the darkness—"Captain Herrera came about Fox." There was an ache in her voice.

"Go home." Dave took the coat out of her hands and hung it on her shoulders. "If your mother-in-law should half wake up and try to smoke a cigarette . . ."

"I'm going." But she held on a moment, gazing up at him, troubled. A lot of questions were in her eyes. She was too tired to ask them. When she turned to call to Phil, Dave said:

"He can't hear you. I'll explain. Run along."

She went, tottering in ridiculous pointed-toed, flame-colored shoes. A minute after the car's tail-lights faded among the orange trees, Phil turned and slammed the trowel into the empty pail. He scowled into the dark.

"God damn it, Gretchen, where's the next bucket?"

Dave found the switch. The mixer motor banged, coughed and quit. "No more buckets," Dave said into the silence. "Come down, Mundy. It's all over."

Phil stood very still. "Who is that? Where's . . .?" Then, expressionless, he moved, quick and sure, along the shaky plank to the ladder. He came down it fast and easy. He didn't look at Dave. He headed for the machine. "You shouldn't have stopped it. I've got a lot more to do." He reached for the flywheel.

Dave caught his arm. "Too much," he said. "You've run out of time. Anybody in his right mind would have left town hours ago. No forwarding address."

Phil didn't hear him. "Before it rains again."

"I'll see they get the word."

"Who?" Dully, still staring at the machine.

"Whoever takes over. Chalmers Company, I expect."

"He's dead," Phil said. "Where's . . . Gretchen?"

"Your mother's drunk again. I sent Gretchen home to look after Buddy. I would have sent her home anyway. She wouldn't want to hear this."

For the first time Phil looked at Dave. With a kid's face waking. "Hear what?"

"The true story of Phil Mundy. Who hated being the bastard son of the town's wartime glad girl. Who had brains and ambition. Not too much of the first, far too much of the second. Who was going to show them all. Who was going to beat the man he worked for at his own game. Who married what he thought was a lot of money, only to find out her grandfather wasn't about to part with any of it. Not to Phil Mundy, the boy who was smart with figures. Nor her father either."

"Fox would," Phil said. "He would have. It was Thorne. She hated me for marrying Gretchen. Fox was the only one in my life who didn't spit on me."

"So you couldn't get the money you thought you'd married. And you were in trouble. Because to start this place—to show Gretchen what a fireball she'd be getting if she married you—to start this place you embezzled money from Chalmers. Right?

I don't know how much, but too much for you to replace on your own hook."

"They'll tell you," Phil said in a dead boy voice. He sat down on the hard gray tire of the mixer. "Tomorrow. The state auditors. They wouldn't have been in for another six weeks. If Lloyd hadn't been killed." He hung his head again.

"It made you very sick, didn't it," Dave said. "Learning you were going to get caught just after you'd made sure of the money. By killing Fox Olson."

Phil's head snapped up. Panic in the blue eyes, dumb panic. "I didn't. I never did."

"You intercepted a letter from him meant for Gretchen. I don't know all that was in it. But one thing I'm sure of. His address was in it . . . his address in Bell Beach. Much as he probably wanted to—I gather he was a goodhearted guy—he couldn't give you the money living. But dead he was worth fifty thousand dollars to you."

"No." Phil stood up. "No. You can't prove it."

"There's a mark on your jacket, where you leaned on the rail of the pier to throw the gun in the water. The paint is old. It's flaking off. And you tracked sawdust there. Police labs can get you coming and going."

Phil's eyes were almost empty now. The hard, sweated muscles hung like meat in a market. The words fell out of a loose mouth. "He was going to kill himself anyway. That was why he had the gun out, cleaning it. He felt good when I came. He thought nobody gave a damn. 'Let's get out of this room,' he said, 'let's take a walk,' and he put a note on the door. I put the gun in my pocket . . . He was going to kill himself anyway."

"So that made it all right?"

The intelligence went away. "I didn't do it." Then, very fast and very surprisingly, there was a hatchet in his hand. He squatted for it, came up with it and swung it at Dave's head in the same single motion. Dave ducked, rammed his head into the boy's belly, grabbed his knees, lifted. Phil's head slammed back against the mixer barrel. Dave felt him go limp. The little ax dropped. The boy slumped to the ground.

Dave tied him up with surveyor's twine and went to get Herrera.

22

He reached home at seven, dropped his clothes, fell into bed. He expected nightmares. None came. Maybe because they couldn't hope to compete with actual persons living and dead. He woke with afternoon sun in his face. He wasn't alone. Anselmo lay next to him, small, naked, warm. He had wanted twenty-four hours of uninterrupted sleep. He ought to have repossessed that key. Anselmo kissed him with a hungry child's mouth. He still smelled of incense.

"You need a shave," he said.

Dave muttered, "Surgery patients get shaved. Not rape victims." Numb with sleep he turned, took the boy in his arms, returned the kiss. "This is a mistake, Anselmo. I warned you before."

"I got a very hard head." Anselmo laughed softly. He propped himself on an elbow and looked down into Dave's face with black solemn eyes. "Don't worry about it. I got to do it with you once. I got to. After that you can say no, if you want to."

"Oh, sure." Dave nodded gravely. "It will be much easier then."

"Aw . . ." Anselmo lowered dark lashes. His small finger traced a circle in the hair on Dave's chest. "I don't mean to be bad for you."

"Go ahead." Dave pulled him down. "Be bad for me."

Anselmo was in the shower and Dave was shaving when the doorbell buzzed. He was naked. He grabbed a flannel shirt and tucked its tails into old corduroys and went to the door barefooted. It could only be Madge. Her feelings wouldn't be hurt if he ran her off on some pretext. It was Madge. But not only.

"Davey?" She breezed in, pulling off gloves. Smart in lean Scotch tweed. "It's cocktail time. And this is Miss Levy."

Miss Levy was a surprise. She fit exactly Dave's twenty-year prescription for what ailed Madge. She was past thirty-five, plain and slightly cross-eyed. But she had a nice smile and good taste in clothes and after she'd shaken Dave's hand her gaze went to the books and records. Knowingly.

"Well . . . uh . . . it's nice to see you," Dave said.

Madge cocked a quizzical eyebrow. But Anselmo answered her question. He started singing in the shower. Loud and clear. "'All the lonely people . . . where do they all come from?'" Dave looked at the ceiling. But Madge began to talk. Fast. She steered Miss Levy far away to look at the Andy Warhol silk-screen in the dining space. Dave closed the bedroom shutter doors.

"Care to join me in the kitchen while I make magic with gin and things?" He hustled them ahead of him, Madge eyeing him without amusement.

"What a stunning kitchen," Miss Levy said. "The

whole house. It's like something out of a magazine."

"Several magazines," Madge said. "Several times."

"Rod Fleming designed it." Dave got ice. "He was a friend of mine." He rattled cubes into a narrow pitcher and heard the shower stop. "Uh . . . excuse me for a second, will you?" He put the pitcher into Madge's hands and started past Miss Levy. "If you want to carry on, the gin is down there in—"

Too late. Anselmo came into the kitchen. Running. Naked. "Listen, Dave. Now let's do it like—" His grin vanished. He tried to stop. He skidded on the wax bricks and sat down, mouth open, water trickling down his smooth brown Aztec face out of his black mop of hair. His eyes got very wide. "Oh, shit," he whispered. He looked at Madge. He looked at Miss Levy. He looked at Dave. Then he scrambled to his feet and ran.

"Uh . . ." Dave said.

"We appear . . ." Madge set the pitcher down. She spoke lightly but with edge. ". . . to have arrived at an awkward moment. Shall we beat an orderly retreat?"

"Look, Miss Levy," Dave began. "Into even the best-ordered households—"

But Miss Levy sidled past him and fled.

"Don't try to explain." Madge caressed his face in passing. With menace. "I'll think of something." She retrieved gloves and bag from a chair. "Though it won't be easy." Her look said he was a traitor and a hypocrite. "'Find someone your own age,'" she quoted him. "'Someone of your own background.' Hah!" She followed Miss Levy into the sunshine. And paused. "Look at that gorgeous car."

He looked. It came slowly up the street, rumbling like a big cat's purr. Red. Low slung. A Ferrari. He shut the door and ran for the bedroom. Anselmo was staring out the window, zipping his tight little flowered pants.

"I am sorry," he said. "I didn't know. . . ."

"Forget it." Dave kissed the dark wet hair.

Anselmo hugged him and nipped his throat. "Let's do it some more."

Dave laughed. "There's someone else coming now. We not only can't do it some more. I'm going to ask you to split."

"Aw . . ." But he gave a little shrug then and sat on the floor and tugged on the soft fringed boots. He stood and stamped and his eyes were round and solemn. "Anyway . . . thank you for doing it with me once."

"No, don't do that. Don't thank me."

"It . . . wasn't good for you too?" Anselmo worried.

"It was very good." The boy had draped his beads on a lampshade. Dave took them down and hung them around his neck. He turned him by the straight little shoulders, opened the door to the patio. Anselmo didn't go.

"But him," he said, "the one with the crazy car. He will be good for you, no? He looks like Rod."

Dave said, "He looks like Rod. The rest I don't know yet." The buzzer sounded. "*Adios, querido.*" He gave the hard little butt a pat. And Anselmo

197

went, small and silent and not looking back. For a bleak moment Dave stared after him. Then he went to open the front door.

"I tried your office," Doug Sawyer said. "I found a Mr. Brandstetter all right. But he wasn't you."

"I'm glad he sent you," Dave said. "Come in. Drink?"

"*Merci.*" Sawyer followed him to the kitchen. "According to Captain what's-his-name—he of the little black cigars—I'd have come to a bad end if it weren't for you."

While he poured ice-melt from the pitcher and replaced it with gin and vermouth, Dave said, "When you came in Ma Kincaid's back door calling his name, I decided you hadn't killed him. It made me wonder who had."

Sawyer watched him turn the ice with a glass rod. "You make it sound simple."

"It was crude"—Dave took glasses from the freezer—"but not simple." He poured and handed Sawyer a glass. No olive. Rod had hated olives.

"Thanks," Sawyer said. "May I take you to dinner? It's not much in the way of repayment for having one's life saved."

"It will do for a start," Dave said.

If you enjoyed this novel, we think you'll like the other books in the Dave Brandstetter series:

Death Claims
Troublemaker
The Man Everybody Was Afraid Of
Skinflick
Gravedigger
Nightwork
The Little Dog Laughed
Early Graves
Obedience
The Boy Who Was Buried This Morning
A Country of Old Men

"After forty years, Hammett has a worthy successor" *The Times*

"Hansen, one of the best practitioners of the California private-eye school . . . writes crisply with a lean, spare prose that echoes Hammett, Chandler and Macdonald" *Washington Post*

"In Brandstetter, Hansen has developed a sympathetic character of depth and integrity"
Chicago Sun-Times

"Hansen writes about Southern California with the descriptive love once given it by Raymond Chandler" *Herald Examiner*

"An excellent craftsman, a compelling writer, he has a real gift for storytelling—for character, for scene, for pace independent of violence"
New Yorker